T... ...wn,
peeling ... ...**nd her**
le... ...ed if she
**still never wore anything under
her nightgown.**

He growled. Why would she wear a white nightgown? So very virginal and innocent.

Who was she trying to kid?

Marina was nowhere near a virgin. She was a sorceress. He should leave now, while he had the chance, before he was tempted to do something he might regret.

But he could not force his feet to move. He could not turn away. Instead he stayed and watched while she was hit by the spray of a wave crashing below, watched while she flung her arms out wide and laughed as brazenly as the weather, watched while her damp white gown turned transparent—and knew that he had no choice.

Knew he had to go to her.

DESERT BROTHERS

Bound by duty, undone by passion!

These sheikhs may not be brothers by blood,
but they are united by the code of the desert.

Their power and determination is legendary and
unchallenged—until two beautiful Jemeyan princesses
threaten their self-control…

In Trish Morey's exciting duet searing passion and
sizzling drama are about to be unleashed!

In May you met:

Zoltan and Aisha

Will this barbarian sheikh tame
his defiant virgin princess and claim his crown?

This month meet:

Bahir and Marina

Infamous billionaire Bahir Al-Qadir risks it all in a
high-stakes game of love!

THE SHEIKH'S LAST GAMBLE

BY
TRISH MOREY

MILLS & BOON

First published in Great Britain 2012
by Mills & Boon, an imprint of Harlequin (UK) Limited.
Harlequin (UK) Limited, Eton House, 18-24 Paradise Road,
Richmond, Surrey TW9 1SR

© Trish Morey 2012

ISBN: 978 0 263 89097 6

Harlequin (UK) policy is to use papers that are natural, renewable and recyclable products and made from wood grown in sustainable forests. The logging and manufacturing process conform to the legal environmental regulations of the country of origin.

Printed and bound in Spain
by Blackprint CPI, Barcelona

Trish Morey is an Australian who's also spent time living and working in New Zealand and England. Now she's settled with her husband and four young daughters in a special part of South Australia, surrounded by orchards and bushland and visited by the occasional koala and kangaroo. With a lifelong love of reading, she penned her first book at the age of eleven, after which life, career and a growing family kept her busy until once again she could indulge her desire to create characters and stories—this time in romance. Having her work published is a dream come true.

Visit Trish at her website, www.trishmorey.com

Recent titles by the same author:

DUTY AND THE BEAST *(Desert Brothers)*
SECRETS OF CASTILLO DEL ARCO
FIANCÉE FOR ONE NIGHT
THE HEIR FROM NOWHERE

CHAPTER ONE

BAHIR Al-Qadir hated losing. For a man barred entry to more than half the world's casinos for routinely and systematically breaking the bank, losing did not come often or easily. Now, as he watched yet another pile of his chips being swept from the roulette table, the bitter taste of loss soured his mouth and a black cloud of despair hung low over his head.

For three nights now he had endured this run of black fortune and still there seemed no end to it. And not even the knowledge that roulette was a game designed to give the house the edge was any compensation. Not when he was used to winning. How ironic that Lady Luck had deserted him now, just when he had been counting on a stint at a casino to improve his mood. He might have laughed at the irony, except right now he was in no mood for laughing.

Still, he managed to dredge up a smile as placed his last pile of chips on a black square, and glanced the way of the croupier to let him know he was ready. So what that he had already dropped the equivalent of a small nation's gross national product? He was nothing if not a consummate professional. The back of his neck might be damp with perspiration and his stomach roiling, but he'd be damned if any of the vultures around the table watching him come undone would read how bleak he felt right now on his face or in his body language.

The croupier called for any more bets even when he would have known there would be none. One by one the other players had dropped out, content to watch the unthinkable, to watch Bahir—the famed 'Sheikh of Spin'—lose, until there remained only him and the numbered wheel.

With a well-rehearsed flick of one wrist, the croupier sent the wheel spinning; a flick of the other sending the ball hurtling in the opposite direction.

A feeble and battered thread of hope surged anew. *Surely this time? Surely?*

Bahir's gut clenched as the ball spun. The damp at his collar formed a bead that ran down his back under his shirt. And, despite it all, he forced his smile to grow more nonchalant, his stance more relaxed.

'Rien ne va plus!' the croupier announced unnecessarily, for nobody looked like making another bet. Everybody was watching the ball bounce and skip over the numbered pockets as the wheel slowed beneath it.

Finally the ball lost momentum and caught in one of the pockets, fighting momentum and bouncing once, twice, before settling into another and being whisked suddenly in the other direction. He knew exactly how it felt. He'd felt hope being ripped right out of him in much the same way for three nights running now. Surely this time, on his last bet of the night, his luck would change? Surely this time he might regain some tiny shred of success to take with him, to show him his gift hadn't abandoned him completely?

Then the wheel slowed to a crawl and with sickening realisation he saw: *red*, the colour rendering the number irrelevant.

It was done. He had lost.

Again.

He thanked the croupier, as if he had dropped no more than the price of a cup of coffee, ignoring the shocked murmurings of the onlookers, intending to walk out of here with his head held high, even if he felt like dropping it into his hands. What the hell was wrong with him?

Bahir didn't lose.

Not like this. The last time he had suffered a run like this...

He pulled his thoughts to an abrupt halt. He wasn't going down that path. The last thing he needed to think about on a night such as this was her.

She was the damned reason he was here, after all.

'Monsieur, s'il vous plaît,' came a smooth-as-silk voice alongside him, and he turned to see the shark-faced Marcel, the host the casino had assigned to him tonight. The perfect host up until now, keeping both his distance and his expression free of the smugness he was no doubt feeling, Marcel had meantime ensured that he had wanted for nothing during his stint at the table. 'Sheikh Al-Qadir, the evening does not have to end here. If you wish, the casino would be only too happy to extend you credit to prolong your entertainment.'

Bahir read his face. The man's bland expression might tell him nothing, but there was an eagerness in his grey eyes that made his skin crawl. So they did not think he was done with his losing streak yet? A momentary challenge flared in his blood, only to be quashed by the knowledge that all he'd done here since he'd entered this establishment three days ago was lose. So maybe they were right. Which gave him all the more reason to leave now.

Besides, he didn't need their money. He had won plenty of that over the years not to be worried about dropping the odd million, or even ten for that matter. It wasn't the money he cared about. It was losing that did his head in. It pounded now, the drums in his head beating out the letters of the word: *loser*. He smiled in spite of it. 'Thank you, but no.'

He was halfway across the room before Marcel caught up with him. 'Surely the night is still young?'

Bahir looked around. A person could certainly think that here. Locked away under the crystal chandeliers, surrounded by luxurious furnishings and even more luxurious-looking women, and without a hint of a window to indicate the time of day, it was possible to lose all concept of time. He glanced at the watch on his wrist, realising that, even leaving now, daylight would beat him to bed. 'For some, perhaps.'

Still his host persisted. No doubt he would be amply rewarded if he hung onto his prize catch a while longer. 'We will see you this evening, then, Sheikh Al-Qadir?'

'Maybe.' *Maybe not.*

'I will arrange a limousine to collect you from your hotel. Perhaps you will have time for dinner and a show beforehand? On the house, of course. Shall we say, eight o'clock?'

Bahir stopped then, fingers pinching the bridge of his nose, trying to produce enough pain to drown out the thunder in his head. Not for the first time was he grateful he hadn't accepted the casino's oh-so-generous offer of accommodation in-house. There were advantages in turning down some of the casino's high-roller benefits. The ability to come and go as he pleased, for one.

He was just about to tell Marcel where he could shove his limousine and his show when he saw it—a flash of colour across the room draped over honey-coloured flesh, and a coil of ebony hair held by a diamond clip—and for a moment he was reminded of another time, another casino.

And, damn it all, of another woman; one he had come here expressly to forget. He shook his head, wanting to rid himself of the memories, feeling the blackness inside of him swell to bursting point, feeling the rush of heat from a suddenly pounding heart.

'Shiekh Al-Qadir?'

'Go away, Marcel,' he snarled, and this time the pin-striped shark took the hint and with a hasty goodnight withdrew into the sea of gowns and dinner suits.

It wasn't her, he realised on a second glance, it was nothing like her. This woman's face was all square jaw and heavy brow, her lips like two red slugs framing her mouth, that honey skin more like leather. And, of course, how could it have been her? He'd left her with her sister in Al-Jirad and surely not even someone as irresponsible as she was would abandon her family so soon after the trouble they had all gone to to rescue her from Mustafa?

Then again, knowing Marina…

He cursed under his breath as he headed for the exit.

What the hell was wrong with him tonight? The last thing he needed to think about was *her*.

No, that was wrong. The last thing he needed to think about was her honey skin, and how she'd still drawn him like a magnet, in spite of the passage of time and despite the hate-filled chasm that lay between them. Yet she'd stepped out of that desert tent and he'd still felt the tug in every cell of his body. What was it now—three years? More? Yet still she'd managed to make him hard with just one glance from those siren's eyes, a glance that had turned frosty and cold the instant she'd realized just who one of her rescuers was.

Still she'd moved like liquid silk, mounting the horse like a natural, her limbs as slender as he recalled, her body still willowy slim despite time and the two children he knew she'd borne.

He might be on the losing streak from hell, but he would bet everything he had that her satin skin was just as smooth as he remembered it to be, whether it be under his hands or in the long slide of her legs wrapped around him.

Curse the woman!

He would not think of her or her long limbs and satin skin! There was no point to it. She was trouble, past or present. She was the worst kind of gamble, the wager lost before the wheel was even spun.

A doorman nodded and bade him a good evening as he passed, even though the night sky outside was already softening to grey. He looked to the cool morning air for the balm it should have been to his overheated skin and fractured nerves, searching for the promise of a new day.

Instead he felt only frustration. He rolled his shoulders on an exhale, protesting the unfamiliar stiffness in his back and neck. When before had his muscles ever been bound so tightly? When before had his spirits ever felt so bleak?

But he already knew the answer to that question. He didn't want to go there either.

He curled into a waiting limousine and tugged his bow tie loose as he sagged against the upholstery, suddenly weary of the world, suddenly restless with his life. He'd thought the casino would liven his spirits. Instead, his luck had let him down and ground him further into the mire.

He looked vacantly out of the window, past the palm-lined esplanade, over the white-fringed sea. Monaco was beautiful, there was no doubt, and justifiably a magnet for the rich and famous and those who craved to be. But right now Monaco and the entire south of France seemed stale, empty and utterly pointless.

No, there was nothing for him here.

He needed to get away, but to where? Las Vegas? No, that would be pointless. Casinos in the States offered even better odds for the house. And he was still unwelcome in Macau after his last winning streak.

An image formed unbidden in his mind, a recent memory of desert dunes and a golden sun, heavy, hot and framed between palm trees as it dipped inexorably lower towards the shimmering horizon.

The desert?

He sat up straighter in his seat, his interest piqued, though wondering if he was mad in the next moment. His recent visit to Al-Jirad had reunited him with his three old friends, Zoltan, Kadar and Rashid. It had also brought two brief forays into the desert. But neither of them had afforded more than a taste of the desert as they had raced to retrieve first the Princess Aisha and then her sister, Marina, from the clutches of the snivelling Mustafa.

The first excursion he had found exhilarating, speeding with his three friends in a race against time across the dunes. The second he'd found less so, although the horses had been just as willing, the company just as entertaining and the sunsets and dawns just as magnificent. It was seeing Marina again after all these years that had spoilt that trip for him.

Of all the women in the world, how unfortunate that Zoltan had to marry *her* sister, the one woman he had sworn never to see again in his life. Even more unfortunate that she could still make him hard with just one look.

Maybe a return visit to the desert would cure him. Maybe the desert sun would sear her from his brain, and the crisp desert night air clear all thoughts of her once and for all.

And maybe not just any desert. Maybe it was just time to go home.

Home.

How long since he had thought of the desert as his home?

How long since he'd called any place home?

But why shouldn't he go now? There was nowhere he needed to be. He had no one to please but himself. And this time he could take the time to drink in the colour and the texture of the desert, take the time to linger

and to observe and absorb its sheer power, and breathe
in air turned pristine under the heat of the desert sun.

But, more than that, out in the desert there would
be no flashes of colour across a crowded room; no
glimpses of flesh to remind him of another time and
another woman he wanted to forget.

He breathed deeply, content for the first time in days,
making a mental note to check flights and make enqui-
ries after he had slept. He was glad this run of nights
was behind him. Surely now this run of bad luck must
be over too? For right now it could not get much worse.

The mobile phone vibrated in his pocket. He hauled
it out, curious who would be calling him at this early
hour, less surprised when he checked the caller ID. He
pressed the phone to his ear. 'Zoltan, what can I do for
you?'

He listened while the grey of the dawn sky peeled
away to pink and his run of bad luck took a turn for
the worse.

CHAPTER TWO

'No.'

'Bahir,' his friend insisted, 'just listen.'

'Whatever it is, I don't need to hear it. The answer is still no.'

'But she can't travel home by herself. I won't allow it.'

'I thought Mustafa was cooling his heels in prison.'

'He is, but I made the mistake of underestimating him once before. I won't do the same again. So long as there's a possibility someone out there is still loyal to him, I'm not taking any chances with Aisha's sister's safety.'

Bahir raked one hand through his hair. 'So get Kadar to do it.'

'Kadar has urgent business in Istanbul.'

He grunted. 'How convenient. Rashid, then.'

'You know Rashid. He's disappeared. Nobody knows where or when he'll show up again.'

He had to be dreaming. Bahir pinched his nose until sparks shot behind his eyelids but there was no waking up. This nightmare was real. 'Look, Zoltan, it doesn't have to be one of us! What's wrong with getting one of the palace guards to babysit her?'

'They're busy.' A pause. 'Besides, Aisha specifically asked that you do it.'

He hesitated. He'd liked what he saw of Zoltan's new bride. Although he'd had his doubts at first, now he could not imagine a better woman as a match for his friend. In any other circumstances, he would not hesitate to do whatever she asked of him. But Aisha had no idea *what* she was asking of him. 'Aisha was wrong.'

'But you know Marina.'

'Which is exactly the reason I'm saying no.'

'Bahir—'

'No. Isn't it enough that I agreed to come with you to rescue her? Don't push me, Zoltan. Why don't you do it yourself, if you're so God damned keen on her having an escort home?'

'Bahir,' came the hesitant voice of his friend at the end of the line. 'Is something wrong?'

'Nothing is wrong!' *Everything is wrong.* 'Listen, Zoltan, we broke up for a reason. Marina hates me and, when it all comes down to it, I'm not that overly fond of her. She might now be your sister-in-law, but you don't know her like I do. She's as irresponsible as they come, the original party girl who's never done a thing for anyone else. She's spoilt and headstrong, and if she isn't given exactly what she wants she goes out and takes it anyway, regardless of the consequences. And, if that's not enough, she's got the morals of an alley cat and the litter to prove it. I tell you now, Zoltan, I am not going back there.'

'God, Bahir, I'm not asking you to marry her! All you have to do is make sure she gets home safely.'

'And I'm telling you to find someone else.'

There was silence at the end of the line. A brooding silence that did nothing to encourage Bahir to think he was swaying his friend's opinion. 'You know, Bahir,' his friend said at last. 'If I didn't know better…'

Bahir felt like growling. 'What?'

'Well, anyone who didn't know you better might actually think you were actually—*worried*—about spending time with Marina.'

'Are you suggesting I'm afraid?'

'Are you?'

'You just don't get it, Zoltan. Even if I agreed to take her, there is no way this side of hell freezing over that she'd agree to come with me. Didn't you hear me say that she hates me? If you'd bothered to ask her you'd already know that.'

There was a telling pause at the end of the line and Bahir felt a glimmer of hope as he saw a way out of this madness.

'In that case, you might try asking her. She'll give you the same answer I have. No. If you're so convinced she needs someone to make sure she's safe, then you find someone else to do your babysitting.'

'And what if she agrees?'

He laughed out loud. 'No way. She'll never agree. Not in a million years.'

'And if she does, will you do it?'

'It's not going to happen.'

'Okay—so, if she says no, I'll find someone else and if she says yes, then you'll do it?'

'Zoltan… There's no way…'

'Is that a bet?'

'She won't say yes.' She wouldn't. If there was one

thing in this world he could be certain of, it was that she would want to be with him even less than he wanted to be with her. Especially after the way they'd parted. 'I know she won't.'

'In which case,' Zoltan said, 'you've got nothing to worry about.'

'No way!'

'Marina!' Aisha called as her sister jumped up from the garden seat where they'd been sitting together. 'Just listen.'

'There's no point,' she said, striding swiftly away. 'Not if you're not going to make sense.'

Aisha chased after her. 'Zoltan and I don't want you going home alone, surely you can understand that? You should have an escort. It's the least we can do.'

'I'll be fine. It's not that far.'

'Like you thought you'd be fine on the way here too, remember?'

Marina shook her head. 'Mustafa's been put away. And this time I won't go overland, okay? Put me on a private jet. Nothing can possibly go wrong.'

'You're going on a private jet, no question, but you're not going alone. Not this time.'

'Fine! So assign me a bodyguard if you must. But I will not go with that man! It was bad enough to find him waiting for me outside Mustafa's tent. If I hadn't known everyone was afraid for me, I would have gone right back inside again.' And it had had nothing to do with the shivers that had skittered across her skin at finding him amongst the party of her rescuers; nothing to do with that flare of heat she had witnessed in his eyes, before they had turned hard, and as cold and unflinching as ice.

Aisha studied her sister. 'You didn't seem that upset when you arrived back at the palace. "A blast from the past", you called him. I got the impression that whatever had happened in the past, it wasn't that serious.'

Not serious. Marina flung her arms out wide, her fingers flicking the flowers of a nearby jasmine creeper in the process and sending its heady scent swirling into the air. She shook her head, reining her arms in and weaving them tightly around her midriff. 'You were all so worried about me, and happy I was safe, how could I make a fuss? Besides, I thought it was over, that I'd never see him again. And clearly he was just as relieved himself that it was over.'

And when she saw the question in her sister's eyes, she added, 'Didn't he take off for Monte Carlo that very same day? No doubt so that there was no chance he could run into me again while I was at the palace.'

'Oh, Marina, I had no idea.' Aisha slid a hand beneath one of her sister's tightly bound arms and coaxed her into a walk through the fragrant garden. 'What happened between you two?'

What hadn't happened? Marina dropped her head, the weight of painful memories dragging her spirits with it. 'Everything and nothing. It all came to nothing.' She frowned. No, not nothing. She still had Chakir. 'I was stupid. Naive. I flew too close to the sun and it's no wonder I came crashing down.'

'Okay. So you had an affair that ended badly, right?'

And this time it was Marina's turn to squeeze her sister's arm. 'I'm sorry, Aisha. I'm not making sense,

I know. But you're right. I met Bahir one night at a party—eyes across a crowded casino, the whole boring cliché, I guess.'

She looked intently at her sister, trying to make her understand. 'But the attraction was so intense, so immediate, and I knew in that instant that we were going to spend the night together. And one night turned into a week and then a month and more, and it was reckless and passionate and didn't look like ending. And I really thought I loved him, you know. I actually thought for one mad moment—maybe more than just one—that he was the one.' She sighed, staring blankly into the distance. 'But I couldn't have been more wrong.'

'Oh, Marina, I'm sorry. I had no idea.'

'How could you? It wasn't as if I was ever home to share my news. And we seemed to have so little in common back then. You seemed content to stay in the family fold while I was continually rebelling against it. Our brothers provided the necessary heir and spare and our father made no bones about it. I figured I was surplus to requirements and so I might as well enjoy myself.'

'A redundant princess,' Aisha said softly to herself, remembering another time, another conversation.

'What did you say?'

She smiled and shook her head as they resumed walking. 'Nothing. It's funny how different we are. But there were times I envied you your freedom and the fact you got to choose your lovers. There were days I wished I could be more like you, headstrong and rebellious, instead of bound by duty. But I guess they both have their down sides.'

'Amen.' Marina sighed and turned her face to the

heavens. 'And now you're married to one of his best friends. Small world, isn't it, when someone who has told you to get out of their life for ever suddenly turns up on your doorstep? Oh, Aisha, I can't go with him. Don't make me go with him!' Tears pricked at the corner of her eyes with the pain of the past. Tears rolled down her cheeks with the complexities of the present and her fears for the future. 'What a mess!'

'He must have hurt you so very much.'

'He hates me.'

'Are you sure? He was there when they rescued you.'

'I doubt that he wanted to be. The others would have expected it, that's all.'

Aisha nodded. 'It's true they are close. Zoltan told me they were the brothers he never had. But hate you? People say things in the heat of the moment—stupid things—but they don't mean them, not really.'

Marina shook her head, her lips pressed tightly together until she could find the words, the burden of her secret suddenly too heavy to bear. 'Oh, he hates me. Even if he had forgotten how much, he will surely hate me when he discovers the truth.'

Aisha stopped walking and turned to her, fear in her eyes. 'Discovers what truth?'

Marina looked at her through eyes scratchy and raw, and her soul bleaker than at any other time in her life. 'The truth about his son.'

Her sister's mouth opened wide. 'Oh no, Marina, surely not? Is Chakir Bahir's child?'

She nodded.

'But you told everyone you didn't know who the father was.'

Marina put a hand to her mouth. 'I know. It was easier that way. And nobody had any trouble believing it.'

'I'm so sorry!'

'Don't be. I had a reputation as a party girl and it came in handy. It made it easier to hide the truth. It was easier to pretend it didn't matter.'

'Even from Bahir.'

'He has no idea.'

Aisha's feet stilled on the path, her gaze fixed on nothing, and when she looked up at her sister Marina was afraid of what she saw in her eyes. 'I think you need to get on that plane. With Bahir.'

Marina pulled back. 'I won't go with him. I can't face him.'

'But you have to tell him.'

'Do I?'

'Of course you do! You have let him know that he is a father; that he has a child.'

She shook her head. 'He doesn't want to know.'

'He has a right to know. It is right that you tell him. And you must tell him. You have no choice.'

'He won't want to hear. He never wanted a child.'

'Then maybe he should have thought about that.' Aisha gave her sister's shoulders a squeeze. 'I'll tell Zoltan it's all set.'

'No! I only told you so you would understand why I can't see him again. I would never have told you otherwise.'

Her sister smiled, a soft and sad smile. 'I think you told me because you already know what you have to do. You just needed to hear it from someone else.'

* * *

Knowing Aisha was right didn't make boarding the Al-Jiradi private jet any easier. No easier at all when she'd seen the plane land and knew he was already waiting inside. How Zoltan had managed to talk Bahir into this was anybody's guess. He would not be happy about it; of that much she was certain.

'You can do this,' Aisha said as she gave her older sister a final squeeze. 'I know you can.'

Marina smiled weakly in return, wishing she believed her, and waved one last time before disappearing into the covered stairs leading to the plane. Right now her legs were so weak and her stomach so tightly wound, it felt like if it snapped she would spin right off the stairs. A fate infinitely preferable, nonetheless, to being enclosed in the cabin of an aircraft with Bahir.

But it had to be done. For more than three years she had wrestled with the question of whether to tell Bahir of Chakir's existence. At first it had been easy to say nothing, the pain of their break-up still raw, the savagery of his declaration never to have children still uppermost in her mind. Why should Bahir be informed of his child's existence, she'd reasoned, when he'd told her he never wanted to see her again? He would not thank her for discovering that, no matter what either of them wanted, they were bound together via the life of a child they had jointly created.

Then, when Hana had come into the world, there had been plenty to think about, and the question of Bahir's rights to know had been easy to ignore. Suddenly mother to two fatherless children, why complicate matters with the father of only one? And Bahir had made it clear he was not a family man; he didn't want her or a child and they certainly didn't need him.

But she'd had reason to wonder lately as she'd watched her young son grow and turn from baby to toddler to young boy, and she'd found herself wondering what Chakir himself would want.

She swallowed back on a lump of apprehension that had lodged in the dry sandy desert that was now her throat. So despite Bahir telling her that he never wanted a child, and even though she was more than happy to accept that as his final word on the topic, maybe for the sake of their son's wishes this would be worth it. For Chakir's sake.

Please God, let it be worth it.

She managed a tremulous smile for the cabin attendant who welcomed her to the plane. Then she was inside the cool interior and he was there, standing with his back to her at a rack filled with magazines, seemingly oblivious to her presence. She wished she could be so oblivious to his, but she could not.

Just the sight of him was enough to make her heartbeat skip and her skin tingle while she sensed a pooling heat building between her thighs. She cursed her body's wayward reaction and wished she could look away. Damn the man! When would she ever be able to look at him and not think of sex? After all the things he had said to her, after the way they had parted, after all the years that separated them, still he conjured pictures of tangled sheets, tangled limbs and long, hot nights filled with sin.

Then again, how was it possible not to think of sex when it was some kind of god that filled your vision?

Was there some kind of formula for masculine perfection; some ratio of leg-length to height or shoulder-width to hip? Some magic number that nature had allocated at conception that marked a man for physical supremacy?

If so, this man was it, and that was just the view of his back.

He turned then, as the attendant ushered her to the seat across the aisle, and the blast of resentment in his eyes made her catch her breath and forget all about magic numbers.

'Bahir,' she uttered in acknowledgement.

'Princess,' he said sharply on a nod before he returned his attention to sorting through the rack. She was amazed he'd managed to pry his jaw apart enough to form the word, it had been so firmly set.

The cabin attendant chatted cheerily while she settled Marina into her wide leather seat, but Marina caught not a word of it, too consumed by Bahir's reaction, too stunned to think about anything else.

So that was what she would get—the silent treatment.

Clearly Bahir was as resentful of being in her company as she was being in his. Equally clearly, he was in no mood for small talk.

Which suited her just fine.

So long as she could eventually find the words to tell him he was a father.

He tried to focus on the business magazine he'd selected from the rack but the words were meaningless scrawl, the article indecipherable, and he tossed it aside. Hopeless. It was no different from the online journal he'd been reading since he'd boarded the jet in Nice, his attention riveted not by the words he was attempting to read but by a simmering resentment that bubbled faster and more furious the closer the plane got to Al-Jirad. Why the hell had he agreed to this again? He still wasn't sure he had agreed. But Zoltan had called and said she'd agreed to go with him and he knew he would have looked weak if he'd refused again.

Much better to look like it didn't matter a bit.

Except that it did.

Because right now, as the attendant stowed Marina's hand luggage and made her comfortable, and as he tried to pretend she wasn't there, his focus was still held captive by the images captured on his retinas—those damned eyes, her pupils large, catlike and seductive. The jut of her collarbones in the vee of the open neck of the fitted ruffled shirt that flirted over her curves, and the jewel-studded belt hugging her swaying hips.

He growled, his nostrils flaring. He picked up his laptop again, determined not to give in, trying to find focus instead of distraction. Because, if it wasn't enough that his mind was filled with images of her, now he could smell her. He remembered that scent, a blend of jasmine, frangipani and warm, wanton woman. He remembered the taste of it on her glistening, sweat-slickened skin. He remembered pressing his face to the curve of her throat and drinking it in as he plunged into her sweet depths.

He shifted in his seat and slammed the computer shut as the plane started to taxi to the runway. How long was the flight to Pisa—three hours? Four? He growled again.

Too long, however long it took.

* * *

How did you find the words to tell someone he was a father? Not easily, especially when that man sat across the aisle from you, rumbling and growling like a dark thundercloud. Any moment she expected to see lightning bolts issuing from his head.

And that was before she had managed to find the words.

What was she supposed to say? *Excuse me, Bahir, but did I ever tell you about our son?* Or, *Congratulations, Bahir. You're a father, to a three-year-old boy. It must have somehow slipped my mind...*

The plane came to a halt at the start of the runway and she glanced across the aisle to where he sat, his posture closed off, his expression grim. Even though she let her gaze linger, even though she was sure he would be aware, still he refused to look her way.

And she wondered how, even if she could find the words, was she supposed to tell him about his child when he wouldn't even look at her?

Did he hate her that much?

How much more would he hate her when he learned the truth?

The engines whined, preparing for take-off, echoing her own nerves, spun tight by his presence, and spun even tighter by the search for the words to tell him.

She closed her eyes and let the jet's acceleration push her deeper into her seat, forcing herself to relax as the whine became a scream and then a roar as the plane launched itself and speared into the sky.

It wasn't as though there was a rush. They had four hours of flight time and then a two-hour drive to her home in the most northern reaches of Tuscany. Why tell him now and spoil the fragile if tense cease-fire that seemed to exist between them? For he would not remain silent once he knew. He would be intolerable. Perhaps with a measure of justification. Still, why make their hours together more difficult than they already were?

No, there was plenty of time to tell him.

Later.

They were an hour into their flight when they were given the news. One hour of interminable and excruciating silence, filled with the static of all the things that were left unsaid, until the air in the cabin fairly crackled with the tension, a silence punctuated only when the smiling flight attendant came to top up their drinks or offer refreshments.

But this time she had the co-pilot with her and neither of them was smiling.

'So fly around it,' Bahir said after they'd delivered their grim message, too impatient for this trip to be over to tolerate delays, whatever the reason.

'That's not possible,' the co-pilot explained. 'The storm cell is tracking right into our path. And the danger is we could ice up if we try to go over. The aviation authorities are ordering everyone out of the area.'

'So what does that mean?' Marina asked. 'We can't get to Pisa at all?'

'Not just yet. We're putting down at the nearest airport that can take us. We'll be beginning our descent soon. Just be prepared as we skirt the edges of this thing that it could get a bit rough. You might want to keep your seatbelts fastened.'

Bahir usually had no trouble sitting. He could sit for

hours at a stretch when his luck was with him and the spinning ball might have been his to command. But right now he couldn't sit still a moment longer.

He was up and out of his seat the moment they'd gone. God, if it wasn't enough that he had to spend six hours in her company, now he would be forced to spend even more time. He raked clawed fingers through his hair. And with her sitting there, her legs tucked up beneath her and those eyes—those damned eyes—looking like an invitation to sin.

'The co-pilot suggested keeping your seatbelt fastened.'

He ignored her as much as it was possible to do. That was the problem with planes, he realised. There was not enough room to pace and to distance yourself from the thing that was bugging you, and right now he sorely needed to pace and find distance from the woman who was bugging him.

Besides, any possible turbulence outside the plane was no match for what was going on inside him. He turned and strode back the other way, covering the length of the cabin in a dozen purposeful but ultimately futile strides, for there was no easing of the tightness in his gut, no respite.

Suddenly he understood how a captive lion felt, boxed and caged and unable to find a way out no matter how many times it turned to retrace its steps, no matter how hard it searched.

'The co-pilot said—'

'I know what he said!' he spat, not needing input from the likes of her.

'Oh, good. Because I thought maybe you'd developed

a hearing problem. I should have realised it was a problem with your powers of comprehension.'

'Oh, I've got a problem all right, and it begins and ends with you.'

She blinked up at him, feigning innocence. 'Did I do something wrong?'

Suddenly the turbulence inside him exploded. He wheeled around and clamped his hands on the arms of the chair either side of her, his face occupying the space hers had been just moments before. He almost grunted his satisfaction, because he liked the way she'd jumped and pressed herself as far back as she could in the chair. He liked knowing he'd taken her by surprise. And, strangely, he liked knowing she wasn't as unaffected by his presence as she made out. 'What do you think you're playing at?'

Inches from his own, those rich caramel eyes opened wide enough until they were big enough to lose yourself in. He watched them, knowing the dangers, watching their swirling depths as she tried to come up with an answer. He'd lost himself in those eyes once before, lost himself in their promises and their persuasion. But that was before, and for all their seductive power he sure as hell wouldn't let that happen again, no matter what pleasures they promised.

'I don't know what you're talking about.'

He shook his head, not believing. 'Then maybe I should spell it out for you. I'm talking about being stuck here—you and me. I expressly told Zoltan I wouldn't do this. I told him there was no way you would agree. And yet here we find ourselves, together. How did that happen, do you suppose? Unless *you* agreed to it. And

I have to ask myself, what possible reason could you have for doing that? What were you thinking?'

She tried to hide her nervous swallow, but he missed nothing of the tiny tilt of her chin and the movement in her throat. He had trained himself to spot the tiniest shift in facial expression or body language of his opponents, a skill that had stood him in good stead through many a poker game. He knew she was hiding something. Did she imagine that there was a chance for them again? Did she think that, because he'd accompanied Zoltan and the others to Mustafa's camp, it meant something? That he was ready to take her back?

She looked up at him, all wide-eyed innocence. 'You think I really want to be here, imprisoned thousands of feet above the earth with you and your black mood?'

Her words were no kind of answer, and he would have told her, only he was suddenly distracted by a stray strand of hair that looped close to the corner of one of those eyes. 'Somebody must have agreed,' he rumbled as he raised one hand. 'And it sure as hell wasn't me.' She flinched as his fingers neared, holding her breath as he gently swept the hair back, surprised when he felt a familiar tremor under her skin, disturbed even more when he felt a corresponding sizzle under his own.

Abruptly he pushed himself away and stood with his back to her, rubbing his hands together to rid himself of the unwelcome sensation. 'Don't you think I've got better things to do than waste my time babysitting a spoilt princess?'

'I absolutely agree,' she said behind him. 'I'm quite sure there's a casino just waiting to be fleeced by the famous Sheikh of Spin. I can't imagine how you managed to drag yourself away.'

His hands stilled. He didn't need any reminders of why he wasn't still at the roulette table. He turned slowly. 'Be careful, princess.'

She jerked up her chin. 'That's the second time you've addressed me by my title. Is it so long that you've forgotten my name? Or can you just not bring yourself to utter it?'

'Is it so long that you've forgotten that I said I never wanted to see you again?'

'Maybe you should have thought of that before you turned up outside my tent that night.'

'Is that what this is about? Why should that change anything? Or were you merely hoping to thank me?'

'Thank you? For what?'

'For rescuing you from Mustafa.'

'Oh, you kid yourself, Bahir. You weren't there for me. You were along for the ride, only there to have fun with your band of merry men. A little boys' own adventure to whet your taste for excitement. So don't expect me to get down on bended knees to thank you.'

A sudden memory of her on bended knee assailed him, temporarily shorting his brain, just as her mouth and wicked tongue had done back then. Not that she'd been thanking him exactly that time. More like tasting him. Laving him with her tongue. *Devouring him.* In fact, if he remembered correctly, he'd been the one to thank her...

He shook his head, wondering if he would ever be rid of those images, knowing he would miss them in the dead of sleepless nights if they were gone. But that minor concession didn't mean he welcomed their presence *now* while he was trying to make a point. 'I wouldn't want your thanks anyway. If I did anything that night, it was out of loyalty to Zoltan and my brothers. It was duty, nothing more.'

'How very noble of you.'

'I don't care what you call it. Just don't go thinking that I've changed my mind about what I said back then. You'd be kidding yourself if you did. What we had is over.'

'You really think you have to tell me that? I have no trouble remembering what you said. Likewise, I have no trouble believing you mean it now, just as you meant it then. And, for the record, it is you who are kidding yourself if you think I am insane enough to want you to change your mind. After what you said to me, after the way you treated me, I wouldn't take you back if you were the last man left on earth!'

He sat back down in his seat. 'So we understand each other, this is merely duty. Of the most unpleasant kind.'

Her eyes glared across at him as he buckled up. 'Finally you say something I can agree with.'

Her agreement offered no satisfaction. His mood only mirrored the darkening sky as the plane descended judderingly through the clouds, icy rain clawing at the windows, the tempestuous winds tearing at the wings— and a sick feeling in his gut that, whatever the weather, things were not about to improve.

CHAPTER THREE

The plane touched down somewhere on the coast of western Turkey at a small airport not far from where the rocky shoreline met the sea. It was almost dark now, although still only mid-afternoon, and they emerged from the plane into a howling wind that tore at their clothes and sucked the words from their mouths. A waiting car whisked Marina and Bahir through the immigration formalities before surprising Marina by heading away from the airport.

She flicked her windswept hair back from her face and looked longingly back at the airport. 'Shouldn't we stay with the plane?' she asked, concerned. 'So we're ready to take off when the weather clears?'

Was it the lashing from the rain that had eroded her harsh demeanour and left her softer, almost vulnerable? Whatever. With her long black hair in wild disarray around her face, and with her eyelashes still spiked with the air's muggy atmosphere, she looked younger. Softer. Almost like she had when she'd woken sleepily from a night of love-making. All that was missing was the smile and the hungry glint in her eyes as she'd eagerly climbed astride him for more.

'Didn't you hear the pilot's last announcement, princess?' Bahir asked, dragging his thoughts away from misspent days and nights long gone. This was the reason he'd never wanted to see her again. Because he knew she'd make him remember all the things he would never again enjoy. 'Airports all over Europe are closed. We are not going anywhere tonight.'

'But my children… I promised them I would be home tonight.'

Bahir looked away. He wasn't taken in by her sudden maternal concern for her children. It was the first time she had even mentioned them and, if they meant so much to her, why had she left them at home in the first place? Maybe in hindsight it might have been the right thing to do this time, given how she had lumbered into the path of Mustafa, but she could not have known that would happen. And surely they had deserved to be at their own aunt's wedding if not the coronation of Zoltan himself?

'We leave at first light,' he said, already looking forward to it. 'You will be home soon enough.' Though never soon enough for him.

She was silent as they passed through a small town that was seemingly abandoned as everyone had taken cover from the storm, the shutters of windows all closed, awnings flapping and snapping in the wind.

'So where are we going now? Why couldn't we stay with the plane?'

'The crew are staying with the plane. It is, after all, Al-Jiradi property. They will not leave it.'

'So we must?'

'There is a small hotel on the coast. Very exclusive. You will be more comfortable there.'

'And you?'

'This is not about my comfort.'

If there was comfort in this hotel, it was proving elusive to find. There was luxury, it was true: the plushest silk carpets, the finest examples of the weaver's art. The most lavish of fixtures and fittings, from the colourful Byzantine tiles to the gold taps set with emeralds the size of quails' eggs.

But comfort was nowhere to be found. Just as it was impossible to sleep. Even now, when it seemed the worst of the storm had passed, lightning still flashed intermittently through the richly embroidered drapes, filling the room with an electric white light and bleaching the room of colour. But the atmosphere in the room remained heavy with the storm's passing, and the soft bed and starched bed-linen felt stifling. She looked longingly at the doors that led onto the terrace overlooking the sea.

Ever since they'd arrived she'd locked herself away in her suite, wanting desperately to find distance from that man. He'd been impossible on the plane, sullen and resentful at first, openly explosive when the news had come of their flight's delay, as if it had been all her fault.

Maybe it was. She had been the one to agree to him seeing her safely home, but it wasn't for the reason he was thinking—that she somehow imagined that he might change his mind, that he might take her back.

What kind of arrogance led a man to believe a woman would want him back after the things he'd said to her?

Did he think she had no pride?

No, the man was unbearable.

So she'd taken refuge in her room, savouring her privacy and her time alone to call Catriona and explain about the delay. She took her time to talk to each of her children and tell them she would soon be home to hug and kiss them and tickle their tummies until they collapsed with laughter again.

It had seemed such a good idea to lock herself away like this while the storm had raged all around. But like the worst of the storm, hours had passed, and still she could not sleep. Still, she could not make sense of the war going on inside herself.

For she hated him, didn't she? Hated him for the way he had amputated her from his life as quickly and decisively as if he'd been slicing a piece of fruit—as if she had never meant more than that to him. Yet still one sight of him and some primal, some base, bodily response kicked in and she had been wet with wanting him. Even now her body ached with need, as if he had flicked some kind of switch and turned her heartbeat into some kind of pulsing drumbeat of desire.

What kind of woman did that make her?

Was she mad? Or simply wanton? The party princess out for nothing but a good time and not caring who it was who gave it to her.

God, it was hot! The mattress seemed to cocoon her, trapping the heat of her thoughts and slowly roasting her in them. She pushed herself up and a bead of sweat trickled from her hair down her neck.

So much for a refuge. All she'd succeeded in doing was exchanging one kind of prison for another. And, in a few short hours from now, she'd be back on the plane—with him—and the torture would continue.

Another flash of lightning lit up the room, and her gaze went to the doors again. There was a chance they could be opened now, without being blown off their hinges or she being blown away herself. And maybe it would be cooler outside on her terrace. Maybe the wind would tear away some of the heat from her overheated skin, and maybe the air might have a chance to cool her sheets while she was gone.

She slid from the bed and reached for her gown, only remembering then that it was still tucked somewhere deep in her luggage because she had thought the weather too warm to need it. She thought for a moment of the hotel robe waiting neatly on a hanger in the closet, but the thought of towelling against her skin when she was already so hot…

She hesitated only a fraction of a moment. She didn't really need it. It was three in the morning, and she was only stepping onto the darkened terrace. She wouldn't be outside for long, and she so craved the feel of cool air and rain on her skin.

The wind had dropped but still she had to hang onto the door lest it slam open. She snicked it firmly closed behind her, knowing the sound would not carry over the waves crashing on the nearby shore, the wind already whipping her hair around her face and sending swirls of air up the slit in her long nightie, brushing against her legs and fanning against her heated core.

She shivered, not with cold from a sprinkling of rain, but with the wind's delicious caress against her skin, and she turned into the onshore wind, pushing against it until she reached the balustrade overlooking the sea.

This was more like it. The shoreline was thick with dancing foam, bright white against the inky black of sea, the tang of salt heavy in the moisture-laden air. In the distance the storm rumbled and lit up the world for an instant at a time.

Then a wild wave crashed on the rocks below and she was hit with the spray, the wind turning the droplets icy on her skin.

She gasped as it hit, her body electric and alive from her head to her toes, and she flung her arms out wide and laughed into the wind with the sheer thrill of it. It was wild. It was exhilarating. And she felt free, just like she'd always yearned to be.

Like she had been once, before Bahir had stolen her heart.

He watched her from his doorway, where he had been standing for more than an hour watching the storm boil and simmer away. At first he had not heard her, whatever sound she made whipped away by the wind or lost under the crash of the sea, but then he had caught a movement out of the corner of his eye, a vision of a woman in a long white nightgown. But not just any woman. *Marina.* A ghost from his past, moving across the terrace with bare arms and bare feet while her black hair followed, untamed, blowing riotous and free.

He watched and grew hard as the nightdress was plastered against her body by the wild wind and the rain, against her lush breasts and the slight swell of her belly, against the sweet curve of her mound. Plastered hard against all the places he remembered, and plastered so close that she might not have been wearing anything at all.

The wind tore at her gown, peeling the fabric high around her legs, and he grew still harder wondering if she still never wore anything under her nightgown.

He growled. Why would she wear a white nightgown? So very virginal and innocent.

Who was she trying to kid?

She was nowhere near a virgin. She was a sorceress. She was wanton in bed, hungry and insatiable. She was sinuous and lithe, moved and twisted with a dancer's grace, and he knew he should go. He should leave now, while he had the chance, before he was tempted to do something he might regret.

But he could not force his feet to move. He could not turn away. Instead he stayed and watched while she was hit by the spray of a wave crashing below; watched while she flung her arms out wide and laughed as brazenly as the weather, watched while her damp white gown turned transparent—and he knew that he had no choice.

Knew he had to go to her.

Her gown was soaked with spray and clinging to her, her hair blowing wild where it wasn't stuck to her scalp and skin, and she knew that soon she would feel sticky with salt and think herself insane for doing something so utterly reckless when she should have been trying to sleep.

But for now she felt more alive than she had in months. More awake. More liberated.

She spun around, lifting her sodden hair high to cool the back of her neck as another wave sent spray flying, when lightning illuminated the terrace and told her in a chill bolt of realisation that she was not alone.

'Bahir,' she said, dropping her arms and backing away into the spray, the sound wrenched from her mouth before even she could hear it. But her body needed to hear no alarm. Her body was already on high alert, her breasts straining and peaked against the fine wet fabric of her gown, her thighs tingling with urgency and her feet primed to flee.

She might have tried to run, but his expression stilled her feet, his face a tortured mask, as if he'd battled his inner demons and lost. His eyes held her spellbound, dark and fathomless in a shadowed face, while his white shirt clung to him in patches, turning it the colour of the golden skin that lay beneath.

She swallowed, tasting the salt of the sea, or was it of his flesh? For even here she could feel the heat rolling off him as his body called to hers, in all the ways it had done in the past, promising all the pleasures of the past and more.

'Why?' she asked softly in a lull in the wind, wanting to be sure, wary of trusting the chemistry between them.

'You can't sleep either.' He answered with a statement, without really answering at all.

'I was hot.'

His eyes raked over her, slowly, languidly, and the heat she saw there stoked a fire under her skin that even the effect of the night air on her wet gown could not whip away. As she looked at how his white shirt clung to his skin, moulding to one dark nipple, she realised how she must look to him—exposed. As good as naked. She wrapped her arms around her torso in a futile attempt to cover herself.

She had never had reason for modesty with Bahir. There was perhaps no reason for modesty now. He had seen it all before and more. But she was different now. She was a mother, and pregnancy had left its inevitable marks on her body. Would he notice? Would he care? He had no right to care and she had no need to wonder—yet still…

Then his eyes found hers again and he simply said, 'I feel it too. Hot.' And she knew he wasn't talking about the weather.

He took a step closer, and then another, so she had to raise her face to look up at him.

'You should go,' he said.

'I should,' she agreed, because it was right, and because to stay would be reckless. The last thing she needed was to be trapped outside on a storm-tossed terrace with a man she had never stopped lusting after, even when she had tried to hate him so very much. Even when she knew she should.

But her feet didn't move, even when the wind pushed at her back, slapping the wet gown against her legs, urging her to get out while she still had time.

'You should go,' he repeated, his voice gravel-rough against her skin. 'Except…'

She tilted her head up at him, her senses buzzing, every nerve in her body buzzing. 'Except what?'

'Except, I don't want you to.'

She swallowed and closed her eyes, one part of her

wishing she'd already left so she'd never have heard him utter those words. The other part of her, that wanton part of her that belonged to him for ever, rejoicing that he had.

'I want you,' he said, and she started and opened her eyes as she felt his hands lift her jaw and cradle her face.

Suddenly it was much too late to run, even if she could have recalled a fraction of all the good reasons why she should.

When she looked up at him it was to see him gazing down at her with such a look of longing that it charged her soul, for it had been so long since someone had looked at her that way, and that person had been Bahir. Nobody had ever looked at her the way Bahir had.

But that was before...

'This is a mistake,' she said, some remaining shred of logic warning her as his hand drifted towards her face.

'Does this,' he said as his fingers traced across her skin and she forgot how to breathe, 'feel like a mistake?' And she sighed into his touch, for electricity accompanied his fingers, leaving a trail of sparks in its wake, just like his touch had that moment on the plane when he had reached out to her brow and left her sizzling with the contact.

Maybe not right now, she thought, in answer to his question. But tomorrow or next week or even next month she would realise this was all kinds of mistake.

And then his hand curved around her neck, gentling her closer to his waiting mouth. Some mistakes, she rationalised, were meant to be made.

The wind pounded at her back, and she let it push

her closer to him, meeting his lips with her own and sighing into his mouth with that first, precious touch.

It was like coming home, only better, because it was to a home she'd never expected to find again. A home she'd thought lost for ever.

'Bahir,' she whispered on his lips, recognising the taste and scent and texture of him, welcoming him.

For one hitched, exquisite moment the tenuous meeting of their mouths was enough, but only for a moment. Until he groaned and pulled her against him, his mouth opening to hers, sucking her into his kiss.

She went willingly, just as her hands went to the hard wall of his chest, drinking in his hard-packed body with her fingers, pressing her nails into his flesh as if proving he was real, as if proving this was really happening.

He was real, her fingers told her, joyously, deliciously, delectably real.

And so very hot.

His breath, his mouth, his lips on her throat, the flesh under her hands—all of him so hot. Yet when his hand cupped her breast it was she who felt like she would combust with his fingers kneading her flesh, his thumb stroking her hard, straining nipple.

Then his mouth replaced his hand, drawing her breast into his mouth, laving her nipple through the thin gown, and silk had never felt so good against her skin.

A burst of sea spray shattered over them. The clouds parted to a watery moon and she clung to his head in order to stay upright and not collapse under the impact of his sensual onslaught.

But when his hands slid down her back and cupped her behind, his fingers perilously close to the apex of her thighs and the heated, pulsing core of her existence, she knew her knees would not last much longer. 'Bahir!' she cried, but he had already anticipated her need, knowing what she asked and what she needed instinctively, as he always had.

He cupped her face in his hands and kissed her long and hard, until she was dizzy and his own breathing ragged when he pulled himself away enough to speak.

'One night,' he said, his voice thick with want. 'Just this night. That's all I ask.'

She knew what he was telling her—that he hadn't changed his mind, that he didn't want her as a permanent fixture in his life and that he would never want her love—but he was offering her this night. Or, at least, what was left of it.

Would she take it?

If she were stronger—if she was more like her younger sister, Aisha, who had tamed her own potent sheikh—she'd tell him what he could do with his one night. But she wasn't that strong. And the choice was so unfair.

She could have this one night with him, and sacrifice her principles and her pride, or she could have none. But her pride and her principles would never make her heartbeat trip with just one glance or one gentle touch. They could not take her to paradise and back and all the wondrous places in between. And what were pride and principles when compared to paradise?

One excruciatingly short night of paradise. A few short hours before they had to rise and return to the airport and continue their flight.

Was it worth it?

Oh yes.

And tomorrow she would tell him about their son— and it wouldn't matter if he never wanted to see her again, because she would have this one stolen night to remember.

She looked up into his eyes and could see the impatience there, the urgency and the crippling, demanding need that so echoed her own.

'Just one night,' she agreed, and felt herself swept up into his arms as if she were weightless.

He carried her to his suite at the opposite end of the terrace from hers, and laid her reverentially on a bed that looked just as storm-tossed as the one she had left. The covers were piled in disarray on the floor, the pillows thumped to within an inch of their existence. It thrilled her that she might be responsible for at least some of the heat that had kept him from sleep.

He stood at the side of the bed, his eyes never leaving her as he purposefully unbuttoned his shirt and tossed it to the floor, his damp, golden skin glowing in the thin moonlight. She held her breath as his trousers soon joined it, then even the scrap of silk he called underwear was gone, and he was gloriously naked before her, his erection swaying proud and free.

Her mouth went dry as he knelt with one knee alongside her on the bed, every drop and bead of moisture her body contained heading south, where it pooled and pulsed with aching, burning need.

'You're beautiful,' she told him. Not that it was any surprise, she was merely stating a fact. For she had always thought him beautiful, dressed or undressed, but never more so than like this, when his full potent masculinity was proudly on display.

He touched one hand to the hem of her nightgown at her ankle and smiled, his eyes glinting in the pale moonlight. 'And you,' he began, 'are overdressed.'

CHAPTER FOUR

THAT was how it began, with his hands skimming up her calves, peeling the damp silk from her legs as he pressed kisses to her ankles, to the backs of her knees, to the inside of each thigh.

And, just when she was gasping in anticipation and expectation, he lifted himself and eased the bunched fabric over her hips, sliding his hands up either side of her waist and past her sensitive breasts, freeing her of the gown, before raining kisses on her eyes, nose and mouth, her shoulders, breasts and every part of her. With every silken touch of his fingers, every magical glide of his hands on her skin, every hot kiss of his mouth, her fever built, until a tear slipped unbidden from the corner of each eye.

The moment was as poignant as it was bittersweet. For she had dreamed of a night like this so very many times. She had dreamed of him returning to her, of admitting he had made a mistake, of begging her forgiveness, and in a thousand different ways, in a thousand different scenarios, she had welcomed him back.

She had dreamed of a magical night when he would return and say he was sorry, that he had been wrong and that he loved her. And she would take his hand, place it on her ripe belly and tell him that it was his child inside her, created in an act of love.

Until finally she would realise that he was never coming back, that he would never seek her out. That it was finished.

And yet, even though she knew nothing ultimately would change, he was here now—and even if it wasn't what she had longed for, even if it would never be enough, it was *something*.

'You are the beauty,' she heard him say, and she opened liquid eyes to see him kneeling back and staring down at her, his eyes filled with what looked like worship. Yet still she waited, breathless with wondering if he might still notice the changes to her body since they'd last lain together, the changes that motherhood to his child had wrought. 'So beautiful,' he repeated.

She held out a hand to him to pull him down and end this desperate need. 'Please make love to me, Bahir.'

He surprised her by taking her hand, turning it in his and kissing her palm, saying, 'I will. But first...' before he let her hand go to skim his hands up the inside of her legs, parting them, pushing them apart to dip his head lower.

She gasped when she realised his intention, and not only in anticipation of the pleasures to come. But they had so very little time and she had expected him to take his pleasure as many times as he could. She had not expected him to want to spend his time giving it. Besides, as much as she had missed the pleasures his wicked mouth could bring, it was the feel of him inside her that she craved.

'Bahir,' she cried as he wrapped his arms around her thighs and opened her to him. 'Please.'

But her pleas were answered by the heated swipe of his tongue along her cleft, and the arch of her spine in response. 'Oh God,' she cried as his tongue made magic with every flick, sending her senses reeling with no time to recover before his lips closed on that tiny nub of nerves, drawing her into his mouth and teasing her senseless with the skill of an artisan—a man who knew exactly what she needed and when.

'Please!' she called, knowing she was already lost, not knowing what she called for.

But he knew. At the hitched peak of her pleasure she felt his fingers join his mouth, pleasuring her inside and out and sending her over the brink.

And that was how it ended, in a million shattering ways, in a million different colours. Years of ecstasy foregone forged into one shattering rainbow moment as she climaxed all around him.

He had always been the best, she thought as the tremors rolled away. Nothing had changed, it seemed, she registered in the pleasure-filled recesses of her mind.

He pulled her into his kiss as she returned to earth. She tasted herself on him, tasted hot sex, heated desire and his burning need, and that need fed into hers, needing him inside her now more than ever.

'God, you look sexy like that,' she heard him say as he drew back. 'Do you have any idea how much I want you?'

She smiled up at him and thought through flickering eyelids about protection, was just about to say something, but he was already reaching across her to retrieve his wallet from a side table, extracting a packet that he tore open impatiently with his teeth. 'Just as well one of us is responsible.'

She blinked, the fog in her blown-apart world clearing. 'What did you say?' she asked, not sure she'd heard him right, not sure she'd understood what he'd meant if she had.

He rolled the condom down his length, his erection bucking and protesting its latex confines in his hand. 'I said...' he dropped back over her, nuzzling a pebbled nipple with his hot mouth as he moved his legs between hers '...it's lucky one of us can think straight.'

She stilled, the magic his mouth producing negated by the toxic content of his words. 'You think I'm irresponsible.'

'I didn't say that,' he said, before finding her other breast with his teeth, angling his hips for her centre.

'You did,' she said, squirming her hips up the bed and away from his attempts to join her. 'That's what you meant—that you were responsible because you thought about protection. You said I was *lucky* you'd thought of it.'

'It's not important!'

'It is important, if that's what you think.'

'Marina, don't do this. I didn't mean anything.'

'But you did! You think I'm irresponsible, don't you? Just because you mentioned protection before I did. You assume I was never going to ask.'

'Come on, Marina, you're hardly the poster girl for safe sex.'

'And you're the poster boy, I suppose?'

'I'm not the one with two illegitimate children. I

would have thought you'd be happy not to be lumbered with a third.'

Blood rushed to her head at the sheer injustice in his words, pounding in her temples, a call to war. 'How dare you?' she cried, twisting her body underneath him, pushing at him with her hands and pounding him with her fists, desperate to get away. 'How dare you talk about my children and say that *I'm* irresponsible? Get off me!'

'Listen!' he said, grabbing one wrist before it could find its target on his shoulder. 'What the hell is wrong with you?'

She glared up at him, her eyes blazing. 'That's too easy. *You're* what's wrong with me. I told you this was a mistake. I knew it was. I'm just sorry I didn't realise how big a mistake until now.'

'I wouldn't worry on that score,' he said through gritted teeth as he rolled away and let her go so that she could clamber from the bed and swipe up her gown from the floor. 'It won't happen again.'

She tugged the gown over her head, shrugging, un-caring when she realised that the seams were on the outside, already heading for the door. 'You better be-lieve it.'

If the flight thus far had been unbearable, the flight to Pisa was torturous, the atmosphere so strained that this time even the cabin attendants sensed the tension in the cabin and left them alone as much as possible. The lack of distractions was no help at all. Marina put her book down again in frustration, wondering if this flight would ever end. She'd tried to read the same passage at least a dozen times now and still the words didn't stick.

But how could anything stick in a mind already overflowing with self-recrimination and loathing? She hated that she had let herself fall under Bahir's heated spell last night. She hated that he had peeled away every shred of logic, accumulated wisdom and life experience that she possessed, just as easily as he had peeled her nightgown from her body.

She hated herself that she had let him.

And when she remembered the way she had come apart in his bed, she wanted to curl up and die. Oh God, how could she look at herself in the mirror? But one thing she knew. She would not bring herself to look at him.

Oh, she could hear him across the aisle, shifting in his seat, grumbling and muttering from time to time. She could feel the anger rolling off him in waves—even his warm, masculine scent was infused with resentment—but she refused to look his way. She could not face him knowing what she had let him do.

She squeezed her eyes shut. Still her muscles buzzed with the memories, her tender tissues still pulsing, still anticipating the completion that would now never come.

God, she thought, squeezing her thighs together in an effort to quell the endless—the *pointless*—waiting, but she was every kind of fool. Maybe Bahir was right. Maybe she was irresponsible after all. But not in the way he imagined.

Of course, their arrival into Pisa was delayed, the airport busy trying to catch up after the storm disruption of the previous day, the tarmac crowded with charter planes and passenger buses all jockeying for space.

So, by the time they landed, her nerves were strained to breaking point and she no longer cared that he was the father of her child or that she had agreed to tell him so. She just wanted him to be gone.

'I'm good from here,' she said without looking at him, as her luggage was stowed into a waiting car outside the busy airport. 'I have a driver. You might as well go.'

She was dismissing him? His lip curled, and it was nothing to do with the smell of diesel in the air or someone's pizza remains lying discarded and sweltering in the gutter. 'That's not the way it works, princess.'

She glared sharply up at him then, probably the first time she'd looked at him since storming out of his room early this morning, and he knew he'd rubbed her up the wrong way by reverting to her title. *Tough.* The less personal they kept this, the better for both of them. 'The deal was to see you safely home.'

'I won't tell anyone if you don't.'

'It's not up to you,' he said, tossing his own overnight bag into the trunk alongside her bags, before nodding to the driver to close it. 'And it's not up to me. I made an agreement with Zoltan and that agreement stands.'

'There's no need…'

He pulled open the back door for her. 'Get in.'

'But I don't want you…'

He leaned in close to her ear, close enough so that anyone sitting at the outdoor tables nearby might even think he was whispering sweet nothings into her ear. 'You think I want you? You think I want to be here?

But this isn't about what I think of you right now. This isn't personal. This is duty, princess, pure and simple. I said I'd do this and I'll damned well do it.'

He drew back as she stood there in the open door for what seemed like for ever, looking like she might explode, her eyes filled with a white heat, her jaw so rigidly set it could have been wired in place.

'Any time this year would be good, princess. I know how you're in such a hurry to be reunited with your precious children.' *Not to mention how much of a hurry he was in to be done with her for good.*

Her sorceress's eyes narrowed then, and something he'd swear looked almost evil skittered across their dark surface while her lips stretched thin and tight across her face. 'You're right, this is all about duty,' she said. 'I had forgotten that for a moment. Just don't tell me later that I didn't warn you.'

He didn't bother to ask her what she meant. He didn't want to know. He slammed the door behind her, and after a few words, giving the driver a day off, took the keys and the wheel. There was no way he was sharing the back seat with *her*. At least driving along Italy's frenetic *autostradas* would give him something relatively sane to think about.

It sure beat thinking about her.

He headed the car north towards Genoa and the exit that would take them into the northern Tuscan mountain region where she lived, while she sat glowering behind her dark glasses behind him. Such a different woman than the one who had graced his bed last night.

What had that been all about? What was her problem? Had that been some perverse kind of pay-back, a kind of getting even for him cutting her off all those years ago?

Was she still so bitter that she would seek any chance at revenge, including finding any justification that she could to stop him mere moments from plunging into her?

What other reason? Because she could hardly take umbrage at being thought irresponsible. God, the entire world's media had used that word in reference to her at one time or another, and with good reason. It could hardly be considered an insult. One didn't have to look further than not one, but two illegitimate children to prove that.

The traffic was heavy on the *autostrada*, but the powerful car made short work of the kilometres through the wide valley to the turn-off onto the narrower road that led towards the mountain region where she lived. Discovering that had been a surprise. He'd figured she'd still be living somewhere close to a city, somewhere she could party long into the night before collapsing long into the day. But she had children now. Perhaps she left them with their nanny while she partied. Maybe she was responsible enough to do that. That would be something.

The pace slowed considerably after they'd left the *autostrada*, the road wending its way along a fertile river valley flanked by looming peaks and through picturesque villages, where the corners of buildings intruding on the road, and blind corners that left no idea what was coming towards you, became the norm.

He dodged yet another slow-moving farm tractor. This was clearly an inconvenient place to live. But maybe she didn't come home too often.

He glanced in the rear-view mirror to see her leaning back against the leather upholstery, her eyes still hidden under those dark glasses. But nothing could hide the strain made obvious in the tight set of her mouth.

So she was tired. Who wasn't after last night?

He had no sympathy. None at all. At least she'd enjoyed some measure of relief. Unlike him, who had burned unsatiated all the hours till daylight, and then some just thinking about her spread out on his bed, wanton, lush and, oh, so slick.

He had been just moments from the place he had longed to be ever since she had appeared like a sorceress on the terrace, gift-wrapped in a transparent layer of silk…

'Didn't you hear me?' she said from the back. 'You have to turn left here.' He had to haul the car around or he would have missed the turn completely.

'How far?' he said as the road narrowed to little more than a one-lane track up the side of a mountain and a snow sign warned of winter hazards.

'A few kilometres. Not far.' He wanted to snarl at the news, more anxious than ever, the closer they got to her home, for his duty to be done.

On the *autostrada*, with the power and engineering excellence of the car at his disposal, those few kilometres would have taken no time at all. On this narrow goat's track, with its switchback bends and impossibly tight, blind corners, it was impossible to go fast, and the climb seemed to take for ever. Longer than for ever, when all you wanted was for it to be over.

The tyres squealed their protest as he rounded another tight bend, pulling in close against the mountainside as a four-wheel drive coming the other way spun its wheels just enough to the right that the two vehicles slid past with bare millimetres to spare.

He took a ragged breath, relieved at the near miss. What the hell was she doing all the way up here? It would be hard to find somewhere more remote, and there was no way he could reconcile the Marina he knew—the high-living girl who was as wilful as she was wild and wanton—with somewhere so rustic.

Though he could see why anyone not enamoured of the party world would want to live here. For, as they scaled the mountain, the vistas grew more and more impressive, of ridge after ridge, valley after valley framed by even higher peaks to one side of him and a range of grey-green mountains in the distance.

'Just on the next bend,' she said at last. 'The driveway on the left.' And there was the next surprise as he pulled into the gravel driveway—he wasn't sure what he'd been expecting, but it sure hadn't been this.

The stone villa sprawled down the side of a ridge, its windows looking out to what had to be magnificent views in every direction. Climbing bougainvillea up the walls trailed bright vermilion flowers, a brilliant contrast against the painted yellow walls. He stepped out and looked around, feeling the Tuscan sun on his shoulders. Kinder than the desert sun, he registered, even in the early afternoon when it was at its most potent. Or maybe it was always cooler at this height.

She didn't wait for him to finish his appraisal and open her door, or maybe she was just as impatient as him for this ordeal to be over.

'This is where you live?' he asked as he pulled her bags from the trunk.

She reached for them but he held them firm and her lips tightened again. 'It's my home, yes.' She sighed with the resignation of one who knew he was going to see his duty to the bitter end, and led the way down a set of stairs on one side of the house that led to a crazy-paved terrace and covered pergola. From here the views were even better. Across a valley between the ridges, a small village clung in colourful array against the dense green of orchards and forest, and before them the land slipped away, lush and green, fading through to grey with each successive range.

Then from the house he heard footsteps, squeals and cries of 'Mama, Mama!' before a door flew open and two dark-haired children exploded from the house shrieking and laughing.

'Mama!' cried the first, a boy that collided full force against her legs, a tiny girl behind packing no less a punch as she flung herself at her mother.

He felt a growl form at the back of his throat as she knelt down and wrapped her arms around them, felt his gut twist into knots. So these were her children? It was one thing to know about them—it was another to see them.

He looked away, waiting for the reunion to be over. He didn't do families. He certainly didn't want to think about the implication of hers, of the men she had fallen into bed with so quickly after expressing her undying love to him. So much for that.

'You're home at last, thank the heavens,' he heard someone say. And he swung round to see an older woman of forty-something, wiping her hands on a flour-covered apron, standing at the door, not looking at the tableau in front of her, but squarely at him. She raised a quizzical eyebrow at the visitor before turning to Marina. 'Lunch is almost ready. Shall I set another place?'

Marina kissed each of her children and rose, taking their hands in hers. 'Bahir, this is Catriona, my nanny, housekeeper and general lifesaver. And these,' she said, looking down, 'are my children, Chakir and Hana. Bahir was nice enough to make sure I got home safely,' she said to them. 'Say *ciao* to our visitor, children.'

Nice enough to see her home safely? Not really. But this time he had no choice but to look down at them—such a long way down, it seemed. Neither child said anything. The girl clung to her mother's skirts, her eyes wide in a pixie face, her thumb firmly wedged in her mouth and clearly not impressed.

But it was the boy who bothered him the most. He was looking up at him suspiciously, eyes openly defiant, as if protective of his mother and prepared to show it; eyes that looked uncannily familiar…

'I'm not staying,' he said suddenly, feeling a fool when he realised he was still holding her luggage like some stunned-mullet bellboy. He set the cases down by the door and took a step back. She could no doubt manage them from here herself.

'You—should stay,' Marina said, her words sounding strangely forced, as if she was having to force them through her teeth. 'Stay for lunch.'

'No, I...' He looked longingly up the stairs to where he knew the car was parked.

'You should...' she said tightly, trailing off. There was no welcome in her words, but rather an insistence that tugged on some primal survival instinct. Some warning bell deep inside him told him to run and keep right on running.

But he couldn't run.

The nanny-cum-housekeeper was watching him. Marina stood there, looking suddenly brittle and fragile, and as though at any moment she could blow away, except that she was anchored to the ground by the two sullen-looking children at her hands—the wide-eyed girl and the boy who looked up at him with those damned eyes...

And with a sizzle down his spine he realised.

His eyes.

The high, clear mountain air seemed to thicken and churn with poison around him, until it was hard to breathe in the toxic morass. 'No,' he uttered. 'Not that.'

And he was only vaguely aware of Catriona ushering the children inside and closing the door, leaving Marina standing as still as a pillar of salt, her beautiful features gaunt and bleached almost to white.

'It's true,' she whispered. 'Chakir is your son.'

CHAPTER FIVE

'No!' The word exploded from his lips like a missile, intended to be just as deadly, just as decisive, before he wheeled away, his purposeful strides bearing him to the end of the wide terrace, taking him away from that house—but it was nowhere near far away enough from this nightmare. 'No. It cannot be!'

'I'm sorry,' she said behind him. 'I know it must be a shock.'

He spun back. 'A shock? Is that what you call it? To be told that you have a child who is, what, two years old? The first you have heard of his existence, and you call that a *shock*?'

'Chakir turned three two months ago.'

He didn't want to hear anything of the sort. His brain scrambled over dates and calendars and what he knew of pregnancy timetables. Three years and two months— plus another nine months or so for the pregnancy, if she was speaking the truth. It was dangerously close to the time since they had last seen each other. But the boy could not be his. It could not be possible.

Except how to explain those eyes…?

He sucked in air as he strode backwards and for- wards along the edge of the terrace, fingers clawing through his hair, searching for answers, finding none, only that it was impossible. Just as it was impossible to go back, to unhear what she'd told him and erase those words from his mind, even though it was what he wanted more than anything in the world.

How could it be true? He'd supposedly had a child this past three years and she'd never bothered to inform him of that fact. Why now? Unless…

'So what do you want, Marina?' he said, rounding on her. 'What are you after? Money? Is that it? You need money to fund this house and your lifestyle, and the boy's real father let you down so you saw the opportunity to lumber me with your mistake in an effort to get child support?'

Her hands fisted at her sides. 'Chakir is not a mistake! Don't you ever call *our* child a mistake!'

He pointed towards the house. 'That child is not mine. It is not possible.'

'Why, because the great and infallible Bahir says so?'

'Because I used protection! I always used protection.'

'And unplanned pregnancies only happen to people who are irresponsible, is that right? People like me? Oh, you should hear yourself, Bahir.'

'I never wanted a child!'

'No, I wasn't planning on it either—and yet this baby happened along in spite of everything we did, in spite of every precaution we took, like babies sometimes do. Maybe your gambler's brain might better understand if I put it a different way—we gambled on contraception and we lost. The baby number came up instead.'

He snorted. What did she know of gambling? Of winning and of losing? *Nothing, compared to him.* 'So you have a child. What I don't understand is why you are so desperate to pin it on me? You, who flitted from one man to another the moment I was out of your life.'

She flinched, almost as if he'd physically struck her, stung, no doubt, by the truth in his words. Yet still that defiant chin lifted and she came back fighting.

'I don't understand you, Bahir. How can you begin to doubt that he's yours? You *know* it's true. You saw yourself in his face when you looked at him. I know you did. I saw the moment you recognised it.'

'So there's a resemblance.' He shrugged, his mind scrabbling for an explanation. 'A coincidence. Nothing more. You can't be sure it's mine.'

'I can be sure, Bahir,' she said. 'Because I had just found out I was pregnant that very day I came to you, the day you chose to cut me out of your life for ever.'

'You were pregnant then?'

'I had just found out. I was nervous. Afraid. But excited too. And I thought—I'd dared to hope—that you might be a little excited too.'

'Yet you said nothing about being pregnant.'

'Because there was no point! Not once you'd told me that you weren't interested in my love and to get out of your life for ever. Not once you'd told me you didn't do family and you never wanted children, never wanted a child. Why the hell would I tell you then, when it was already too late?'

He dropped his head onto his fists, his chest heaving with the weight of today's discovery, already buckling under the weight of the memories of the past and of a day so dreadful he had tried to block it from his mind.

'So this is all my fault, is it? You neglect to pass on the fact we have a child, and somehow it's all my fault.'

She took her own sweet time to answer, standing there, looking like some wronged angel when, damn it all, she was not the wronged party here!

Then she sighed. 'No. This is not about finding fault. I'm just trying to explain why I didn't tell you, in words you might understand. You would hardly have thanked me that day if I had told you I was pregnant. You were so vehemently opposed to the idea of children, I could not share that with you. On top of everything else, I could not risk it. I could not risk you telling me what to do…'

He blinked with the realisation of her meaning. She thought he'd have insisted on a termination—was that what she'd been about to say?

He cast his mind back to that day, a day that had always been going to be bleak but a day that had grown progressively worse with the arrival of the mail, a poisoned day that had turned more toxic when she had appeared unexpected and looking like sunshine in a smile. He'd damned well near hated her in that moment. And then she'd asked him if he'd ever wanted a family and the bottom had fallen out of his world.

He'd thought he'd known her. He'd thought they understood each other. Live for the day. Take your pleasure while you could. Party on and then move on.

And it had been good. Better than good.

But then she'd surprised him by turning as needy and grasping as all the others. 'Have you ever thought about having children?' she'd asked. 'I love you,' she'd said. And his mind had turned as fetid and as poisoned as his memories.

She'd known she was pregnant even while she'd been uttering those words.

And if she'd told him that day, if he'd known, would he have insisted on a termination? God. He didn't know. He'd never considered the possibility. It had never been an issue. All he'd known was he'd never wanted a child. But seeing that boy and thinking…

He cursed. Sometimes it was better *not* to think.

'So, why tell me now, if you couldn't tell me then?' he asked, feeling sick with it all, the deceit, the lies, the shock of discovery. 'Why wait until now, nearly four years after the event, to drop this bombshell?'

She shook her head and he tried not to notice the way the ends of the layers in her long hair bobbed around her face when she moved. He hated the way the ends danced and played and caught the sunlight, as if none of this mattered. He hated that he even noticed. 'I didn't want to tell you at all,' she said. 'Not ever. I was happy for you never to know. And you'd told me you never wanted to see me again, so why would I complicate things with news you wouldn't want to hear? That's how I reasoned. But things have happened lately, and—'

'What things?'

'Like you turning up with Zoltan and the others at Mustafa's camp, for a start. I never expected that, not after you'd said you never wanted to see me ever again.'

His jaw tightened. 'I did it for Zoltan and Aisha. I would have done the same for anyone.'

She gave a soft, sad smile. 'Thank you for spelling it out so succinctly, but I'm under no illusions on that score, believe me. What you did was all about duty to your desert brothers. Just as seeing you made me realise that it was my very duty to tell you about your son, no matter how unpleasant that was going to be for both of us. You had a right to know, whether you ever wanted a child or not, whether I wanted you to know or not; it was your right as a father to know that your child existed. Why else would I have agreed to getting on that plane with you?'

'So that's how it happened?'

She paused, that tentative shadow of a smile back on her face. 'Do you really believe I would want you to be the one to escort me home? You were the last person I wanted to be with, and I knew you felt the same about me but I had no choice. How else was I supposed to tell you?'

He sucked in air. 'So Zoltan was in on it too? Did the whole world know before me?'

'No. As far as I know, he knows nothing. Only Aisha knows, and I only told her because she was the one who came up with the crazy idea. She assumed that, because we knew each other before, we'd make the perfect travelling companions. I tried to talk her out of it. In the end, I told her why it wouldn't work.'

'But then you agreed.'

'Aisha helped convince me of what I was already thinking—that you had to be told.' She bowed her head. 'Except, when I got on that plane with you, I still couldn't find the words. You were so angry and I was afraid, and it was easier not to say anything. It was easier to send you away at Pisa and forget about telling you entirely. It was easier…

'But then you insisted on driving.' She shrugged. 'Anyway, it's done now. And, in the end, it wasn't about you. Not entirely.'

'What do you mean?'

'I did it for Chakir. I did it for our son.'

He glanced towards the house. 'You really think the boy cares?'

'Maybe not now, but one day he might. One day he might want to know more about his father, about what kind of man he is. One day he might come looking for you to understand himself and try to work out his place in this world. You need to be prepared for that eventuality.'

'And that's all you want by telling me?'

'Isn't that enough for a man who never wanted a child? A man who already never wanted to see that child's mother again? But now you know. I'll leave it up to you if you want to tell your own family. And I guess…' She crossed her arms, shrugging a little. 'If, say, they wanted to meet him, or a photograph of him or something, you'll let me know?'

'They won't bother you,' he said with grim certainty. 'I know they won't.'

He sighed as he looked around at the wide expanse of view and then back up at the impressive villa. 'Nice place,' he said. *Very nice place for a woman who'd partied on her shoestring allowance for years.* 'Did your father buy it for you? For the children?'

She seemed surprised by the question, blinked and shook her head. 'No. It belongs to a good friend of mine.'

A good friend? The girl-child's father? 'How convenient,' he said.

'I guess you could say that.'

He hesitated, wondering what more there was to say. 'So, that's it, then?'

She looked up him, her arms around her belly, her eyes almost hollow. 'That's it.'

It sounded to him very much like a dismissal, one he was only too happy to accept. 'I have to go. I won't stay for lunch.'

'Yes, of course,' she said, as if she'd expected nothing less. As if she wanted nothing more than for him to be gone. 'Thank you for seeing me home. Excuse me if I don't see you to your car. I should go and see to my children.' And she turned and walked briskly away.

He'd been dismissed. He sat there, the car idling in neutral on the gravel driveway. All he had to do was put the car into first and release the handbrake and he was out of here and away down the mountainside, and he could begin the whole forget-this-ever-happened thing.

That was what he'd intended when she'd calmly walked away. Because if she could calmly walk away from this encounter, then so could he.

Except that he couldn't.

Because this time he wasn't just walking away from her. He was walking away from *him*. The boy. His child? But of course it had to be his child. Just one look in the boy's eyes and it was obvious all the paternity tests in the world would say the same thing.

That the child was his.

He'd seen his own eyes then, just as he'd seen those

of his newborn brother as he'd lain in their mother's arms, all baby wide-eyed innocence. And his father had chipped him on the chin and told him his new brother looked exactly as he had done as a baby. The same dark eyes that looked out at him from every mirror.

The same eyes he saw in the child.

His child.

He thought of his baby brother. Thought of the celebrations that had accompanied his birth, thought of the time with him he'd been cheated of when death had stolen him away with the rest of them. He thought of the amulet he'd found in the lawyer's package, the amulet that had been around his brother's neck when he had died.

And he thought of the child inside the house.

He'd never wanted a child. He'd never wanted family. Never wanted to risk losing what was so very close to him again.

And for so long it had worked. He lost nothing, and when he did, it was only money. He hated losing but it was only ever money.

But now, it seemed, he had a son. A child of his, inside that house, a house she had likely been left by the man she'd moved on to soon after leaving him, if the age of the girl was any guide. Did he want his child raised under such a roof, paid for by just another of his mother's lovers? Surely it should be his money supporting his child. It should be him providing a home to his own.

He might have abandoned all thoughts of having a family, but that did not mean he had abandoned the tenets of the life in which he had grown up.

He was a Bedouin, born and bred.

Family was everything to his people.

So how could he just walk away?

He could not. It was as if Marina had given him a child and then stolen him away in the very next breath. Paying lip service to his parentage. Letting him know like it was some mere formality. That, once she had done her duty in telling him, his role was over.

And that sat badly with him.

Very badly.

He had never wanted a child, it was true.

But now there was this boy. *Chakir*.

And curse luck, chance, happenstance or however it had happened; curse the fact that he was now inexorably tied to a woman he wanted nothing more to do with. He could not simply walk away.

Marina closed the door behind her and leaned against it, taking a deep breath as she wiped the tears from her eyes, hoping to regain some semblance of normalcy before she joined her children for lunch or they would want to know what was wrong and why she was crying.

God, if he'd stayed a moment longer she would have turned into a walking fountain out there. When he'd reminded her of Hana's mother, she'd nearly lost it. All that had kept her together was witnessing the play of expressions on his face. For one who prided himself on his poker face, it had only been too obvious what he had been thinking.

His mind had been working overtime imagining exactly what kind of 'good friend' had lent her this house.

But what of it if she had enjoyed the attentions of some rich sugar daddy? What was it to him if she had

had other lovers who bestowed upon her gifts? She couldn't imagine he had remained celibate all these years. A man of his appetites? Not a chance.

No, all he'd succeeded in doing was giving her all the more reason to be glad he was gone.

And she'd needed that.

Her duty was now done. Bahir knew the truth and it was up to him to deal with it. No doubt, knowing him, he'd disappear back into denial and pretend today's news had never happened.

One could only hope.

She blinked and swiped at her cheeks one final time. It was time to get on with her life.

Time to move on.

Time to put to bed once and for all any forlorn and pathetic hope that Bahir might one day change his mind. How much plainer could he make it that he'd only turned up at Mustafa's desert camp site because Zoltan and his friends had been there? How much plainer could he make his position than by his rapid exit once he'd been confronted with the existence of their son?

Bahir was history. He had no part in her life. Not for the last four years. Not now. Maybe it was time to fully accept that.

From the kitchen came the sound of Catriona serving up lunch to two hungry toddlers, and she smiled softly. It was Bahir's loss that he had turned his back on his child and walked away. Not hers.

She would not let it be hers.

The knock on the door came as they were finishing lunch. A sizzle of premonition down her spine came with it. *Surely not?*

'I'll go,' said Catriona, watching her face, missing nothing.

'No,' she said rising from her seat where she'd been overseeing Hana feed herself. 'I should go.'

'And if it's him?'

Marina gave a smile she didn't come close to feeling. Catriona had asked nothing since she'd returned, though there were questions in her eyes, questions the woman wouldn't ask until the children were asleep and they would have time to talk properly.

'Then he'll want to see me anyway.'

The knock on the door came again, louder and more insistent this time. And something in that knock told Marina that she didn't need to see who it was to know.

'Are you sure?' Catriona asked, collecting plates and keeping her voice light as if nothing was wrong, blessedly keeping the atmosphere in the kitchen on an even keel when Marina's world felt like it was teetering on the edge of a precipice. But the local village woman had a real talent for smoothing the atmosphere, Marina acknowledged, thinking back to when they'd both nursed Sarah those last few months, and how even at the end she'd kept the household together when they could so easily have all fallen apart.

'I'm sure. Don't worry, I'll be right back. It's probably just someone from the village.'

She knew she was kidding herself—anyone from the village would know to come to the kitchen door—even before she pulled open the heavy timber door.

'Bahir,' she acknowledged, stepping out and closing the door behind her as premonition turned to fear. One look in his eyes told her she needed to put as many barriers as she could between this man and her children. For when he'd left, he'd looked like a man defeated, as if he'd had the stuffing knocked out of him. But now he seemed taller and more powerful than ever and, with the cold, hard gleam in his eyes and the resolute set of his jaw, he looked more like a warrior. He looked like the real battle had not yet begun.

Her mouth went dry. He wasn't back because he'd changed his mind about lunch. 'Was there something else?'

'You could say that,' he said, and the chilling note of his delivery made her blood run cold. 'I've come for my son.'

It took a while for the words to register. 'I don't understand,' she said finally, finding no sense in the words; no sense that eased the turmoil inside her. 'What do you mean you've *come* for him?'

'It's quite simple, really. You've had our son to yourself for three years. Now it's my turn.'

CHAPTER SIX

'No,' she managed, her entire body in denial. *'No!'*

'You see,' he continued, as if she hadn't uttered a word, let alone that particular one, 'I've decided it's not enough for me to be some kind of absentee father. If the child is mine, as you are so happy to attest, then I have a responsibility as his father to see that he is raised properly.'

'He is being raised properly! Did he look to you like he is being neglected or is suffering in any way? What are you trying to prove, Bahir? What do you really want?'

'I told you. I want my son!'

She glanced at the house behind her, wondering if Catriona and the children could hear them arguing from inside. 'There's no need to shout,' she warned him, before heading across the crazy-paved terrace, her arms tightly bound beneath her breasts.

'Did you hear me?' he said behind her, his voice lower now but no less menacing. 'I want my son.'

'No. This is madness. You're just angry. You're lashing out, merely wanting some kind of pay-back. Because you can't be serious.'

'I'm perfectly serious. You must have considered the

possibility when you hatched this plan to tell me I was his father that I might actually want a hand in raising my own child?'

She blinked, momentarily struck dumb, because she'd never given a moment's thought to the possibility. It was too fantastical; too unlikely. *Too impossible.* She spun around, hoping he would see the truth of her argument in her eyes. 'But you never wanted children! You were so vehemently opposed to the idea that I was too afraid to tell you I was even pregnant. And now you're telling me that you want a hand in raising him?'

'It's true, I never wanted a child. But what I wanted is irrelevant now, wouldn't you say? Because that child exists. That child is here, and he is mine, just as much as he is yours!'

'But you can't just walk in here and demand your son like he is some kind of package—like a possession to be passed around to whoever it is whose *turn* you perceive it to be.'

'Why not?'

'Because he is not a parcel to be handed from one person to another! He is a child. And because I won't let you take my son.'

He laughed, a short, harsh sound. 'Your son? You seem to have a short memory, princess. Such a short time ago you seemed determined to tell me the boy was mine.'

'He is your son, but you would be no kind of father to him.'

'Has anyone given me the opportunity? How can you be a father to a child you do not know exists?'

'You didn't want to know. You didn't want a child.'

'But the boy is here!'

'His name is not "the boy". His name is Chakir!'

He grunted. 'Something else I was not given a hand in! What other things have you decided for our child, princess? Have you already chosen a school for him? Perhaps he is already enrolled? Have you already procured for him a rich and wealthy bride?'

'Don't be ridiculous.'

'Yes,' he said, his face twisted, his strong features contorted. 'It *is* ridiculous to have to ask when, as the boy's father, I should already know these things. I should have been given a say in such decisions.'

She shook her head, determined not to give ground, no matter how shaky it felt beneath her. 'I didn't think you'd be interested. I didn't think you'd care, given you'd made your position crystal-clear.'

'And so you neglected to tell me he'd even been born!'

She kicked up her chin. 'You didn't want to see me again. I got the impression that meant for any reason.'

'And that…' he paused, the look in his dark eyes damning '…is your pathetic excuse for denying me the knowledge of my own son's existence? That's your excuse for secreting him away for three years?

'And now you think it gives you the right to keep him for ever and only offer me some token parental right, in case one day he might want to look me up?' His chest heaving, he turned and strode away to the balustrade, where the land dipped steeply away below and the valleys and mountains formed his backdrop.

Such a majestic backdrop, she thought, that a mere man should fade into insignificance. No man had a right to look majestic before such a sight. But this man did. He was tall and broad like the mountains themselves, and just as impossible to scale, his true self just as unconquerable and as dangerously unattainable as the mountains' dizzy heights.

And last night—no, this very morning—he had taken her to such dizzy heights with the magic of his mouth and his wicked tongue and she had tasted herself in his kiss...

She shivered. Now this same mouth, lips and tongue told her he wanted to take Chakir. *Her son.* Why would he want to do this other than out of spite? Because he felt slighted? But how could she make him see it, he who was as stubborn and impossible to move as that range of mountains behind him? How was she supposed to fight him?

'It doesn't give you that right,' he said, spinning around, and she blinked and had to rewind the conversation to catch up. 'And now it's time for his father to exercise some of his rights. I want to take the boy home.'

'Home?' She shook her head. When they had been together they had lived in a succession of apartments and hotel rooms always within range of the casino of choice. 'I didn't know you had a home.'

'I am planning to visit the home of my fathers in Jaqbar. I want the boy to come with me. I want to show him the land where his father was raised.'

Jaqbar? Shock punched the air from her lungs. He couldn't have surprised her more if he'd said he wanted to take him to Monte Carlo and teach him all he knew about gambling, for there was nothing in Jaqbar but endless desert. 'You want to take him somewhere out in the desert? You must be insane! You can't take him there! He's just a child.'

'He is my child. And the desert is his home.'

'No, *this* is his home. The only home he knows. Besides, you don't know the first thing about children. You wouldn't know how to raise one properly if they came with a manual, let alone out in some desert somewhere. I won't let you take him. I won't let you take him anywhere.'

'Then I won't give you a choice. We will take this to court if that's the way you prefer to play it, princess. Imagine the fun the tabloids could have with that little custody battle: *Party Girl Princess Steals Baby.* Your father would be so proud of his firstborn daughter on reading that.'

She swallowed, the picture he painted too vivid, the consequences too great. For the first time since the onset of her rebellious adolescent years there were the fragile beginnings of a decent father-daughter relationship between the King and her. He still would never understand the circumstances of her becoming mother to not one, but two illegitimate children. That had been her fault too, for never wanting to reveal the truth, but they were at last coming to some kind of decent relationship.

She could not bear it if that fledgling relationship were threatened. And it was so unfair! 'I never stole Chakir!'

'No. You just stole three years of my child's life from me. His first steps; his first words; his first smile. Did you celebrate his birthdays? I hope you enjoyed them.' He glared at her. 'Enjoyed them enough for the both of us.'

His words bit deep, the accusations hitting home. All those milestones she'd enjoyed and celebrated, she had never once realised were in fact crimes against the absent father. 'You didn't want a child,' she said, more like a whimper, in her crumbling defence.

'You didn't give me a choice!'

'I tried,' she said. 'Don't you think I tried? Don't you remember that day?'

'I remember you asking if I wanted a child. I said no. I don't remember you telling me you were already pregnant.'

She wound hands through her hair, twisting it so tightly it pulled on her scalp, welcoming the pain in the hopes it might blot out some of the emotional pain. But it was futile. 'So we can work something out,' she said, scrabbling for solutions. 'Maybe you could visit some weekends or go out for the day? There's a market every Tuesday in Fivizzano, the village at the foot of the mountain, and there's always the beach at La Spezia. It's not far.'

'Or there's a court in Rome where I will be given full custody of my son when I tell them how unsuitable you are to be a mother to my child.'

Was he serious? He'd actually fight her in court for custody? Her jaw dropped open, her mind stunned by the lengths he would resort to. But who was he kidding? Did he really imagine himself the model father? 'You really believe for one moment that they would give custody to you, a man who has spent most of his life in front of a roulette wheel? A man who doesn't even own a home? Not even the famed Sheikh of Spin could find a positive *spin* in your reputation. You'd be laughed out of court.'

He swatted away her protest with one hand like he was swatting at an annoying insect. 'Then maybe we should put it to the test. Which one of us, I wonder, has the most to lose in going public?'

'You bastard!' she snapped. For there was no question in her mind which one of them would come off worst. She could not risk the exposure and the inevitable muckraking that would follow. And she could not risk anyone uncovering the truth about Hana when she had promised Sarah she would not tell.

Oh God, what if they took Hana? What if she lost them both?

Tears pricked at her eyes. How could he do this to her? Was his need for revenge so great? Did he hate her so very much? 'You wouldn't do it,' she whispered, hoping he would realise he was costing her even just in his threats. 'You couldn't.'

'Of course I would, if you continue to try to keep my child from me.'

'Bahir, please,' she said, shaking her head. 'Don't do this. You can't take him. He doesn't know you.'

'Whose fault is that? Not mine. He will come with me to the desert. I will teach him how to ride and how to hunt. I will teach him the ways of his Bedouin forefathers.'

'But he's just a baby. He's barely three years old. He's too young for such a trip.'

'I was born in a tent in the desert! I grew up there. How, then, can he be too young?'

She couldn't take any more in. She was beyond

stunned—already punch-drunk and reeling from the emotional roller-coaster she had been on for the last twenty-four hours—but this latest piece of news sent her mind spinning. She had spent months with this man and never once had he hinted at his origins. But when had they ever spent their time talking? In the dizzy heights of their relationship, nothing had mattered beyond the two of them and their own private sensual world, filled with the taking and giving of pleasure, and it was only now, when their relationship was already ancient history, that she was gleaning any insight into his past.

But that still didn't mean he could take her son away from her.

'Don't do this,' she said. 'You can't expect to just take Chakir away from me and off to some desert somewhere. You don't know the first thing about children and you're a stranger to him. He would be terrified. And it would be irresponsible of me, as a mother, to simply hand him over to you and let you take him.'

He said nothing, his eyes savage, his jaw grinding together, taking his time as if weighing up the truth in her words. Time she couldn't afford to waste.

'You see,' she argued, 'it won't work. He wouldn't go with you. It would be inhuman do that to him.'

'Fine,' he said at last. 'We'll do it your way. I want the two of you packed and ready to leave by ten tomorrow.'

'The two of us?'

'Of course,' he said, looking at his watch as if suddenly bored with the conversation. 'If it will be so problematic—if the child will not come by himself—then clearly you will just have to come too.'

'No, Bahir,' she said, reeling again from this latest twist. 'That's not what I meant.'

'On the contrary, I think it's an excellent solution.'

'You're forgetting Hana.'

'No. Not the girl,' he said with disdain, as if the topic was closed. 'She stays.'

'I'm not going anywhere with Chakir and leaving Hana behind. I will not leave any child of mine behind.'

'Since when? You, the wonderful mother, seemed only too happy to leave your children at home when you gallivanted off alone to their aunt's wedding.'

'You think I should have dragged them out of their sick beds to go to a wedding half a dozen countries away?'

'Chakir was unwell?'

'They both were, with chicken pox. I wasn't going to bother going to the wedding at all except Catriona insisted I should go. They were both over the worst by then and she said she'd cope. Only now...'

'Only now, what?'

Only now she wished she hadn't gone at all. If she'd stayed at home she wouldn't have stumbled into Mustafa's path and needed rescuing. She wouldn't have needed an escort home and this nightmare wouldn't be happening now.

She sucked in air. It *was* happening and somehow she had to deal with it, somehow she had to find a way through, one that didn't involve him calling all the shots.

One that maybe involved calling his bluff.

'Only nothing.' She looked up at him, fired with new resolve. There was a risk, of course, that she could lose everything with this tactic, but she sensed there would always be a risk where this man was concerned. Far better the one that she accepted than the one he imposed on her.

'Nothing at all. But I tell you this, Bahir. We are a family—Chakir, Hana and me—and I will not leave Hana again so soon. I will not do that to my daughter. Either she comes, or none of us do. And if you don't like it, you can abandon any plans of taking Chakir anywhere, and you can take me to court. And don't expect it to be easy, because I will fight you every step of the way.

'And you can feed whatever twisted, sordid little stories you like to the press and let's just see who ends up with custody when they discover that you have nothing; that you're just a gambler with no home and no life outside of the casino. Who in their right mind would award such a man custody of a child? What kind of father could he ever be?

'So take me to court if that's what you must do, and I will wear the consequences, but don't think you can make blanket decisions that concern *my* family and expect me to blindly fall in with them!'

In the end they all went, including Catriona, who had offered to accompany them, an offer Marina had been only too happy to accept. It wasn't just having someone to help keep an eye the children that she was grateful for, it was having someone along who could be both chaperone and the voice of wisdom should Bahir's constant presence turn her thoughts more carnal—or, worse still, made her think that Bahir might somehow manage to fit into their small family on a more permanent basis. Catriona was no fool. They had had a long heart-to-heart last night while she had explained exactly how the land lay. Catriona would soon talk sense into her if she looked like wavering.

Bahir grunted as he loaded the last of the bags and she handed him a hamper of snacks for the children. 'What have you told the boy?' he asked.

'I've told them that we're going on a holiday. What did you expect me to tell them?'

'You didn't tell him—who I am?'

'I think it's a bit premature for that, don't you? Maybe you might try getting to know him a little first.'

She wandered off as Catriona and the children arrived and he watched the women buckle the wriggling children into their car seats, the older woman climbing up alongside them. That addition to their party had taken him by surprise, but now he was quite happy she was coming. She could look after the girl.

'Where are we going?' asked the boy as Bahir climbed into the driver's seat of the big four-wheel drive. 'What's it called again?'

'Jaqbar,' he said, looking at the child in his rear-vision mirror, noticing for the first time the fading marks on his gold-olive skin. The girl had them too, peeking out from under her dark fringe and on her cheeks. If he had noticed them earlier he would probably have assumed they were mosquito bites. So Marina had been telling the truth about their illness? He hadn't known whether to believe her or whether she'd been trying to shore up that 'good mother' myth that she liked to espouse.

'Is it far?' the boy asked.

'We'll be there in time for dinner,' his mother said.

'So long?'

'Don't forget,' she added, 'there's a plane ride first.'

'I like planes,' Chakir said, as the car headed down the mountain. 'I like it when they take off. Whoosh!' And his hand took off into the air.

Beside him the girl giggled hysterically, pulling her thumb out of her mouth to make her own hand plane. 'Whooth!' And she fell into another burst of giggles.

He caught Marina's sideways glance, and sensed she was wondering how long he would cope with all this. He merely smiled as he pulled to the side to let the blue village bus heading the other way squeeze past. The girl he could do without, it was true, but he'd be damned he was going to let Marina think he could be no kind of father for his own child. He might be a gambler, but he was a professional one, who had made millions from his work. Why should that make him a bad father? He would enjoy proving that he could be the father his son needed.

After all, if she could surprise him with her strength last night in arguing her own case, then he could only return the favour. And she had surprised him, he reflected. He hadn't figured on her fighting back. He'd witnessed her arguments crumbling beneath the weight of her guilt—he'd witnessed her almost defeat—and he'd had her in the palm of his hand.

But then he'd told her the girl wasn't invited and she'd transformed into some kind of lioness defending a prized cub, willing to do anything to do so. And why? What was it with the girl? Why was she so special? Because her father had been special to Marina? Was he the one who owned this house?

He growled at the thought of another man making love to Marina while his child lay neglected in his cot nearby.

So much for all her declarations of undying love.

They landed in the heat of Souza, Jaqbar's capital, shortly before six. 'We stay here tonight,' Bahir said as they transferred to a private villa on a palm-studded resort, the air cooled by the spray from a hundred dancing fountains. 'Tomorrow we journey out to the desert, so you might want to take advantage of the pool. There's not a lot of water where we're going.'

'Where are you going?' asked Chakir, with a child's curiosity. He watched the boy's mother warn him with her eyes, but the boy was having none of it. 'Aren't you coming for a swim too?'

'Chakir,' his mother admonished. 'It's not polite to ask so many questions.'

On the contrary, he liked that the boy was bold and not afraid to ask him questions. 'It's fine,' he said, putting a hand to the boy's head—his *son's* head—only to be hit with a sudden jolt of a long buried memory of his father doing the same to him. His long robes had flapped in the desert wind, his face leathery and lined by the sun, his eyes overflowing with love. And for a moment he was rendered speechless. He blinked, clearing his vision of the memories, seeing his dark-eyed son studying him intently.

He smiled. 'I have some things to organise for the morning, to ensure your camping holiday is the very best one it can be. Maybe later I will be back in time for a swim.'

'We're actually camping?'

'That's right. Just like I did, when I was a boy.'
Although the tents he had secured were a far cry from
the basic squat black tents he remembered as a child.
He would not have Marina say he could not provide for
his son. He looked over at her now, to where she stood
silently watching with something like fear in her eyes.
'We do want this holiday to be perfect, don't we?'

CHAPTER SEVEN

THEY were all in the smaller children's pool when he returned, the children splashing in the shallow water clutching their pool toys, the women close by, ready to reach out a supportive hand if one of the children slipped.

He glanced for a moment at his son, but it was to Marina his eyes were drawn. She was seemingly shrink-wrapped in a red one-piece that showed her long, golden-skinned limbs to full advantage, her black hair restrained in a thick long ponytail that hung, luxuriant, down her back like a heavy cord of silk.

That patch of lycra might have been more than she'd worn two night ago when she'd lain naked and open to him on his bed, but somehow it was also less. For it only accentuated what he knew lay beneath, every glorious curve, every intoxicating dizzy peak, every dip and every dark secret place, so that even now his hands itched to reach out for her, even now his body stirred.

Damn.

She chose that moment to look up and she stilled as their eyes connected, the air between them shimmering, heavy with expectation. Expectation for what? She'd been the one to walk out on him the other night. She'd been the one to walk away. And all ostensibly because he'd implied that she was irresponsible.

Okay, so one of her illegitimate children was his and he might have some responsibility to shoulder for Chakir. But to fall pregnant again so quickly after the birth of his child with another? Hadn't she learned anything?

If not irresponsibility, it smacked of carelessness at the very least.

Was that why she looked at him that way, then, with her eyes like neon signs atop a seedy nightclub promising untold pleasures of the flesh? Because she simply couldn't help herself? Because she looked at every man that way?

He cursed under his breath. She had no right to look at him that way! He balled his towel in his hands and flung it to a nearby lounger before striding to the end of the lap pool. Right now he could do with a cool down, and it had nothing to do with the temperature.

'Bahir!' he heard his son call just before he hit the water. He just kept right on swimming.

Marina sat with her son at the end of the pool waiting for Bahir to finish churning through the water on his seemingly endless laps. But she didn't mind how long he took. First, his preoccupation with his laps had given her the chance to cover herself with her sarong. Something about the way his gaze had raked her body had told her that she needed every bit of protection from his eyes that she could get. Secondly, it had afforded her the time to breathe.

And she had needed the time to remember how to breathe.

For the sight of him dressed in nothing more than a pair of swimming trunks and staring at her like he had done two nights ago just before his head had dipped between her legs had damn near shorted her brain.

It was only luck that he'd dived into the pool when he had or she would still be blindly staring—*wishing*…

The water this end of the pool churned as Bahir's powerful arms sliced a path through and Marina assumed he was about to tumble-turn yet again before powering back the other direction when instead he took another stroke and glided into the wall.

He came up heaving for air, spinning droplets from his hair with a flick of his head as her son—*their son*—jumped up and down at the edge of the pool.

'You swim so fast,' he said in unrestrained awe, and the hero worship in his voice almost broke Marina's heart. He had no heroes in his life, she realised, no male role models close enough to them to make an impact. She bit down on her lip, guilt weighing heavily upon guilt.

Bahir hauled his body from the pool with an ease that belied the work his arms had just done, and she had to force herself to look away and not stare in wonder. 'I bet you can swim faster,' he said to the boy, grabbing his towel and pressing his face into it. 'I'll give you a race right now, if you like.'

Chakir's face crumpled. He shook his head. 'I…' he started, his expression stricken as he struggled with the confession, 'I can't swim.'

'Why not?' His words, intended for the child, were

gentle enough. The black look, on the other hand, was directed squarely at the mother.

She took her son's hand. 'Chakir had a fright when he was two. We thought we'd wait until he was ready before having any more lessons.'

Bahir knelt down and regarded the boy eye-to-eye, a frown marring his patrician brow. 'Is that so?' He looked back at the expanse of inviting pool behind him. 'Tell you what, how about I give you a lesson right now? I bet before you know it, you'll be racing me.'

His eyes opened wide and Marina could see excitement blended with the fear. 'You'd give me a lesson?'

'Of course,' he said, 'but only if you think you're ready.'

Chakir looked uncertainly at his mother. 'Maybe in the shallow pool,' she suggested, trying to encourage.

'But Mama,' he said, puffing out his chest, 'you can't swim there. Not really. Everyone knows that.' She wanted to smile at how brave her boy was being.

'Don't worry,' Bahir said, already leading the boy to the shallow end of the lap pool. 'I'll take good care of him.'

Marina watched on nervously. How would he know how to take good care of a child? He knew nothing of children. But then, as she watched him getting Chakir to kick holding onto the edge of the pool, and showing him how he could relax and float on his back to gain confidence in the water, reluctantly she was forced to acknowledge that he was taking good care of him. When he managed to get him to put his face under the water by himself, she knew it. By the end of the lesson her son even managed to take a few tentative and haphazard freestyle strokes as Bahir supported his body in the water.

As she watched father and son working together, she felt besieged by guilt that she had kept them apart all these years. But there was something more beyond that feeling of guilt, something fragile that bloomed inside her. Something precious that she did not want to put form to, just to feel it was enough.

'Did you see me, Mama?' Chakir said proudly after the lesson was over, running up to his mother, surrounded in plush towel, clutching it at his chin, his teeth chattering in excitement. 'I was swimming!'

'I saw you, Chakir,' she said, embracing him in her arms. 'I'm so proud of you!'

'And I'm having another lesson tomorrow before we leave.'

She shook her head. 'Are you sure he said that? I don't know if there will be time.'

'I'll make time,' Bahir said, catching up with the boy. Once again he was there before her in his swimming trunks and nothing else and this time he was dripping wet. She swallowed, trying not to notice the chest hairs plastered against his skin, forming whorls and patterns. She tried and failed not to notice as they coalesced into a single dark line that trailed southwards to circle his navel before venturing still lower towards those fitted black trunks.

'It's no trouble,' he added. She looked up, her face burning, knowing it was all kinds of trouble trying to think clearly while confronted with such a perfect masculine specimen, especially when your eye was level with his navel.

'Thank you,' she said, standing up as Chakir ran off to tell his sister Catriona was collecting up their things. 'That was good of you.'

He shrugged. 'The boy should know how to swim.'

'But how on earth did you know where to start? You've had nothing to do with children.'

'My father taught me.' And then, before she could pursue that revelation, he asked, 'What happened to him? Why was he so afraid?'

She clutched her arms as she watched her son now showing Hana how to swim, his arms making windmills in the air, and she wondered that Bahir had been able to make such a difference in one short lesson.

'He was just starting to gain some confidence when a boy—the local bully—jumped into the pool while Chakir had his face under the water. I think he only meant to scare him, but Chakir moved and he landed on his back and pushed him right under. He could have drowned.'

She shivered, remembering that day, remembering the panic as his instructor had pulled her lifeless child from the water and she had watched him pump his chest until he had coughed and spluttered and spewed out half the pool.

She sensed him stiffen beside her and turned to see his eyes bleak and cold. 'And then I never would have got to meet my son.'

'No,' she said, realising she'd just racked up one more black mark against her name—but what was one more in her already long list of transgressions? 'I guess not. And now, if you'll excuse me, I must go and help

Catriona with the children. Apparently we have an early start in the morning.'

He watched her go, watching the way her ponytail swayed from side to side with every step, drawing attention to and accentuating the feminine motion of her hips under the sarong she'd wrapped around herself like a suit of armour. It would take more than that for him to not be able to imagine her naked beneath. He watched her go, hating himself for needing to watch.

She must be a sorceress, he wagered, if he could at times hate her with every fibre of his being yet at the same time lust for her so desperately that to throw her to the ground and bury himself deep inside her would not be quick enough.

She had to be.

They did start early, but not too early that Chakir could not have another swimming lesson before their departure. He was full of it as the four-wheel drive headed out of the city and into the wide desert lands, boasting that he would soon be fast enough to beat Bahir.

The motion of the vehicle along the desert highway soon had the two children sleeping in the back seat, Catriona snoozing alongside.

'You handle it well,' Marina said as the car powered through a wide, flat valley, a range of red mountains rising from the rock-strewn desert floor on either side.

'Handle what well?' he asked.

'Chakir and his ambitions to beat you.'

He shrugged a shoulder, his wide brown hands slung seemingly casually over the steering wheel, his eyes alert and constantly scanning the desert ahead for hazards. 'It is good to be ambitious.'

'I'm surprised, that's all. That you take it so good-naturedly.'

'He is a child with a child's sense that nothing is impossible and that everything is attainable, even the stars. I have no doubt I was much the same. Once.'

His words piqued her interest. 'Only once? You don't think that any more?'

'Let's just say I learned the hard way that there are some things the universe will not give you, no matter how much you wish for them.'

'What do you mean?'

He smiled then, if you could call it a smile. 'And you worry that our son asks too many questions.'

'I'm sorry,' she said, falling silent, but not only because of his gentle rebuke. It was the use of the term 'our son' that had stilled her tongue.

Not 'the boy' or 'my son' but 'our son.'

And she surprised herself by liking the sound of it on his tongue, a sound that lit a candle of hope inside her that this did not have to end badly—that they did not have to resort to a heated custody battle, but could forge some kind of truce for the sake of their son.

'He likes you,' she said, musing out loud. 'Especially after the swimming lessons. I think you've made a conquest.'

'Good. I like him too.' He took his eyes from the road again to look at her, and this time they were filled almost with respect. 'You have done a good job with him. He is a fine boy.'

The flickering flame inside her burned a little

brighter. It wouldn't last, she knew enough to know that. Sooner or later she would do or say something that would remind him of the sins she had committed against him and the walls of hostility would rise up between them once again. But right now it was nice not to be at war.

They stopped for a picnic lunch at a tiny oasis, little more than a well and a few hardy palms shading a crumbling mud-brick shelter.

'It's hot,' declared Chakir on climbing from the air-conditioned vehicle into the stifling desert air, then proceeding almost immediately to chase his sister around the well until their picnic was ready, as if totally oblivious to the heat.

'Did someone live here once?' he asked when he had finally collapsed down onto the picnic rug, gasping but ready to eat. He pointed towards the crumbling hut. 'In that building?'

'No,' Bahir answered. 'At least, not all the time. It's a shelter, for shepherds and other travellers passing through. Somewhere protected from the elements when herding sheep and goats on the coldest of nights, and somewhere to take shelter when the dust storms blow in and turn the sky black in the middle of the day.'

Chakir's eyes opened wide. 'Have you ever seen a dust storm?'

'Yes. When I was a boy. The sand blotted out the sun and it was so dark I could not see my hand in front of my face.'

'Were you here for a holiday too?'

'No. I grew up here. Or, not far from here.'

Chakir looked around. 'How could anyone live here, in the desert?'

His father smiled. 'When we get to the camp, I will show you.'

'Will you show me too?' Hana asked, breathless and fascinated and clearly determined not to miss out. 'Please.'

Marina watched the shutters come down in Bahir's eyes. 'I'd like very much to hear too,' she said, adding her support to the chorus. 'We both would, wouldn't we, Hana?'

This time Bahir had no choice but to nod. 'Of course.'

'Why do you do that?' Marina asked later as they loaded the last of the picnic things in the back of the car. 'Why do you answer Chakir's questions in such detail and yet barely grunt when Hana asks something?'

'Do I?'

'You know you do! I know Chakir is the reason we're here, but there is no need to treat Hana as if she doesn't exist.'

'I don't know what you're talking about.'

'I'm talking about the way you try to ignore her.'

'I told you not to bring the girl.'

'And I told you it was all of us or none.'

'Well, you got what you wanted, then. She's here, isn't she?'

'So don't treat her as if she isn't. She's Chakir's sister, whether you like it or not.'

'So maybe I don't.' He climbed into the driver's seat and slammed the door.

She hated him in that moment, hated him with every fibre of her being. Not that he would care. He didn't want anything from her, apart from her son. And now she half-regretted coming. The warm satisfaction of seeing father and son together was waning, for instead of filling a space in her family and providing a father figure for Chakir, the way he was acting could soon drive a wedge between her two children.

It was so unfair, so unjust. Hana had suffered enough in her short life. She deserved happiness too.

And, because she felt like she should make up for his indifference, she caught the girl as she ran puffing up to the car after her brother and swept her up in her arms, spinning her around. Hana squealed and wriggled but she held firm. 'I love you, Hana Banana,' she said, using her pet name for her. 'Never forget that, okay?'

The toddler stopped her wriggling for a moment to hold her jaw in her small hands to kiss her. Her blue-black eyes looked solemnly down at her. 'I love you too, Mummy.' Then she giggled and squirmed to be free.

Very touching, he thought, unable to avoid watching the performance in his side mirror, knowing it was all for his benefit, knowing it was all so false.

For what did she know of love really? She was as fickle and changeable as the desert wind, changing direction and blowing from one man to the next with just as little reason.

No, she knew nothing of love.

The girl proved it.

A herd of ibex scattered as the car topped a rise, the horned goats scampering and leaping at speed in all directions, thrilling Chakir and Hana. Below them lay the camp site, a collection of large tents set around another, more welcoming-looking oasis.

'Wow! Is that where you live?' Chakir asked from the back seat.

'No,' Bahir answered. 'We moved around a lot when I was a boy, but this is not far away from one of the places we camped.' He would not go to that place, now just an empty patch of desert. But a patch of desert that held too many memories and where the mournful wind carried the cries of too many lost souls.

'Are your family there?' Marina asked, a sudden tightness to her voice. When he turned his head he saw she was clutching a pendant at her throat, her eyes filled with fear. Was she worried they would recognise the family resemblance and let the cat out of the bag before she was ready for Chakir to find out the truth about his father? Or was she worried they might try to kidnap Chakir and keep him here for ever?

Whatever, she had no cause for concern. The only people in the camp were those his old friend Ahab had organised to help with their visit, brought in from one of the remaining tribes that still managed to live a simple Bedouin lifestyle despite the call of the modern world.

The simple Bedouin lifestyle, he reminded himself, that he had turned his back on.

'No. They're—not here.' He watched the tension around her expressive eyes ease as she relaxed back against her seat, and he drank in her profile: her dark, lash-framed eyes, her lush sinner's mouth. He wondered why she had to be so beautiful that at times he almost ached to look at her.

He turned away, unable to answer his own question. Not sure he even wanted to try.

The camp grew busier as they neared and their approach was noticed—not 'New York' frenetically busier, or 'Monte Carlo' flourishingly dramatically busier, but *Bedouin* busier, where every movement was purposeful and halfway to poetic. Robed figures swayed rhythmically across the sands, gathering at a point where their vehicle stopped, an impossibly old-looking man at their helm.

Ahab, he realised with surprise as he pulled the vehicle to a halt. He was not arrow-straight as he had always been, but stooped and frail, his face creased with age, his hair bleached whiter than the sands. And it gave him cause to wonder anew about just how long he had been gone. Years he had been away, years that had melded into one long absence, years that knew no numbers.

'Ahab,' he said, alighting from the car to air that brought him up with a jolt, air made of the timeless scent of the desert flavoured with the scent of herbs and roasting meat. Air that made him remember so much that it was a moment before he could embrace his old friend's bony frame. 'It is good to see you.'

'You have come, Bahir,' the old man said, tears squeezing from his eyes. 'You have come home at last.'

Something heavy shifted inside him, like the slide of a weighted box across the deck of a ship in a rolling sea. Uncomfortable. Disarming. He waited, half-anticipating whatever it was to slide back the other direction and right itself, but it stuck fast. When he blinked and told himself to ignore it, Marina and Catriona had the children out of the car and Ahab was smiling down at them through watery eyes.

'Welcome,' he said, after Bahir had introduced the small party, his gaze lingering on Chakir for just a moment longer than it needed to, just a moment that told Bahir that the old man had recognised in an instant what he had so pointlessly tried to deny. 'There is a feast being prepared in honour of your visit, but first I will show you to your tents and then we will sit and have tea.'

Hana and Chakir squealed with delight when shown the interior of the tent they were to occupy. Their low beds were covered with cushions in every bright colour imaginable. The floor was lined with rugs on which sat a toy camp site, complete with tents, camels and tiny people.

Marina was tempted to squeal herself when she saw the room partitioned off for her, lined with silk wall-hangings and the finest, softest carpets with bronze lamps atop carved timber side tables. And the bed? It was every little girl's fantasy but a grown-up version— decorated with sumptuous fabrics in rich jewel colours, bold and beautiful, and surrounded by filmy curtains. A bed fit for a harem. And such a big bed for one.

She thought wistfully about what it would be like to wake up in such a bed in a Bedouin tent in the middle of the desert, in the arms of a Bedouin lover after a night of earth-shattering love-making and with the promise of more to come.

That would make much better use of such a bed.

Her two children burst into the room, wanting to check out her room. Chakir whooped when he saw her bed and launched himself across the room to dive onto it between a gap in the curtains, with Hana in gleeful hot pursuit, her short legs struggling fruitlessly to make the final leap.

She laughed and picked up the squealing girl and jumped onto the bed alongside Chakir, tickling the two of them until tears streamed from their eyes and they begged her to stop. Then she curled her arms around each of her children and they lay there panting, in the big wide curtained bed.

No, she thought as she kissed each of her children on the head, their hair tickling her nose. Such a big bed was not such a waste. Not at all.

They had time to be shown around the camp before the hour designated for their formal welcome, and Hana and Chakir ran gaily from one tent to the next, a clutch of children accompanying them, accepting them in their midst.

But it was the animals that fascinated them the most: the camels and horses the tribe used now for sport rather than transport, and a herd of local goats, black-haired and horned, their new kids bounding in delight. Hana was so entranced with the newborns, it was almost impossible to drag her away.

Soon after, Ahab formally welcomed them at the tea ceremony, the handing over of each cup to their guests an offer of friendship and welcome. Ahab bestowed a special honour on the children, solemnly placing a necklace bearing a pendant of a stylised eye over each child's head.

'What is it?' she whispered to Bahir.

'A token,' he said through a tight throat, unable to

bring himself to believe. 'To ward off the evil eye and keep them safe.' He knew better. Nothing could keep a child safe if the fates chose to take it.

But both children accepted their tokens with the solemnity the ceremony called for, and then the formal part of the ceremony was over and a smattering of children amongst the tribespeople soon drew Chakir and Hana into their games.

As afternoon slipped into evening, they moved to a circle of seats under the darkening sky where a camp fire was already blazing and where three musicians were plucking tunes on their stringed instruments or beating time with their drums. Here they feasted from the endless platters of spiced meats and roasted vegetables, followed by rose-scented sweets washed down with thick, sweet coffee.

It was the perfect evening, Marina thought as she watched her children playing and making new friends, while the air was filled with scented wood-smoke and a haunting song that seemed to expand to fill the landscape.

She watched Bahir talk to Ahab at his side, and she wondered about this place Bahir had brought them to. Wondered again about his family and why they were not here to greet him, when others like Ahab had openly welcomed him home.

Why had he never shared the details of his past?

A bundle of waning energy landed heavily in her lap, short-circuiting her thoughts—Hana, giving up on the game, panting and breathless, her eyelids struggling to remain open.

She cradled the child in her lap, stroking her hair

back from her face. 'Are you tired, Hana Banana? Do you want to go to bed?'

'No,' the toddler said emphatically, rubbing one eye with her fist. 'Not tired.'

'I know,' Marina said, smiling, rocking the child gently in her arms, knowing the exact moment she fell asleep, her head lolling back. She leaned down and pressed her lips to Hana's cheek, thinking of her mother in that moment and wishing that she could be here, a tear sliding unbidden down her cheek.

Mother and child, Bahir thought, listening with one ear to what Ahab had to say, but fully intent on her with the sleeping child in her lap. How could a woman look sexy cradling a child that was not even his? But somehow she managed it. She still had the power to make him burn.

He nodded to Ahab, agreeing on a point as he watched her rise gracefully to her feet, though it could be no easy task to do so with the dead weight of the child in her arms, while Catriona rounded up a weary Chakir.

'You're not leaving already?' Ahab said, rising alongside him.

'It's the children,' she said. 'They've had a long day.'

'I'll stay with them,' Catriona said. 'You come back.'

Bahir rose. She looked so slight and the child so awkward and floppy-limbed. 'Can I help?' he asked, not knowing what that might actually involve.

She responded by clutching the child even closer to her chest, as if she would not trust him with her. 'We'll manage, thank you.'

'We will see you shortly?' Ahab asked.

But it was to Bahir's eyes she directed her gaze, Bahir who felt her uncertainty, her fear and even something like temptation. 'Perhaps.'

'Princess Marina is a fine mother,' Ahab said as the small group padded across the sand towards their tent. 'Her children are a credit to her.'

And, as much as Bahir resented the presence of the girl, and as much as he resented what it meant, he could not disagree.

'Have you gone to visit them yet?' the old man asked a little later as he rose to prod the fire into life, the haunting notes of the stringed *oud* catching on the desert air like a poem on the breeze.

Ahab's question caught him unaware. Bahir didn't have to ask who he meant, but he'd been listening intently for any sound of Marina's return and he had not been thinking of *them*. But he was here in Jaqbar, wasn't he? Wasn't that enough for them? It wasn't as though he could change anything. He shrugged, more carelessly than he felt. 'Is there any point?'

The old man nodded sagely. 'You should go. They have waited a long time for you to come.'

Bahir said nothing, knowing in his bones that the old man was right, that reconnecting with his homeland meant finding his family. But the closer he had come, the more uncomfortable he had felt. After all, what could he tell them? That he might as well have lost his life with theirs for all the good he had done in the world? That he had wasted years of life in the gambling dens of the world?

He could not bring himself to say those things. So

instead, he just answered with the barest inclination of his head and a hand he rested on the old man's bony shoulder, hoping the old man would understand, as Marina returned in a whisper of fabric and a scent that complemented the pristine desert air and made it all the sweeter.

He breathed it in. She was back. And he was relieved, not only because he had been worried she would not return, but because Ahab now had somewhere else to direct his probing questions, affording him breathing space to deal with the demons of his past the way he needed to.

And he *would* deal with them, he thought as Ahab asked Marina about the children and he zoned out, an unswallowable lump in the back of his throat, that sliding weight inside him scraping across his gut at the thought. And, of course, some time he would go.

He owed them that much.

But only when he was ready.

It was late. The musicians had gone and Ahab and the others retired, the fire now a bed of coals. She knew she too should go to bed, but the moon was a heavy golden pearl hanging in the sky, turning the desert into a honeyed nether world, and the air was shimmering with expectation. Expectation of what, she didn't know, except that neither of them seemed willing or able to retire and break this fragile spell that existed between them.

And it occurred to her that, in all the time they had been together, they had never done anything so utterly simple. They had spent time in casinos and ballrooms, and had made love in the bedrooms and bathrooms of some of the most palatial hotels in the world, but they had never enjoyed the simple pleasure of watching a camp fire burn down under a pearlescent desert moon.

He looked beautiful in this light, she thought, stealing a glance when he was staring into the fire. The angles and planes of his face were either lit with a flickering glow or hidden in shadowed mystery.

A face that could still warm her blood with just one glance, so masculinely beautiful that she had to look away. She sighed and lifted her face to the moon, bathing her skin in its brilliance, wanting to drink in the serenity of this moment and hold it close to her for ever, wondering why such a moment should happen upon them now, when it was already too late.

And it was too late. For they had had their time, and it had been amazing, both of them soaring above the world of mere mortals, the sex sublime, the heights of passion reached unimaginable.

Only to be burned up on her savage re-entry into the world.

She closed her eyes, wanting to block out that dark memory. That time was so long ago. And now, for whatever reason, the fates had brought them together again and they had to find a way to move forward.

For now they shared a child.

Dear Chakir, who had turned her life around and made her realise that there was more to life than parties and avoiding responsibilities. For how could you avoid responsibility when you were a mother? You had no choice but to grow up.

The moon felt soft on her face. She would go to bed soon. She had not been going to come back at all, but

Catriona had told her she was far too young to go to bed yet, and there had been something in Bahir's eyes—an invitation? A plea?—and whatever it was had drawn her back, like a moth to the flame, to the fire.

And there had been nothing to fear. Nothing had happened other than they had discovered they could sit in companionable silence around a camp fire and drink in the sounds of the desert night, while tingling with delicious awareness with every breath.

There was something about this woman, Bahir thought as he watched her turn her face to the moon, her eyes closed—something elemental that he had never seen before until that stormy night on the terrace and she had danced when spun in the spray from the crashing waves.

Something that made him wonder if he had every truly known her.

He had always thought her just a good-time girl—and she *had* been then, wild, abandoned and wanton in bed, taking as much as she gave—but there was more to her than that. For she had depths and resources he would never have imagined. And a fiercely protective instinct where her children—one of them his—were concerned.

She was the mother of his child.

His child.

And yet, even though he could see those traits, even though he might otherwise applaud them, the eternal questions still gnawed away at him. Why had she turned to someone else so quickly? How could she have forgotten what they had shared? Out of spite? Or because she had never truly loved him?

It had to be that. What else could it be?

He looked at her upturned face, tracing the noble profile, the high forehead, the delicate uptilt of her nose, the long black lashes that swept her cheek, and those lips that had once been his sensual playground and his alone.

He had to ask himself the question—why had he ever let her go? Why had he let her walk into someone else's arms and someone else's bed?

She sighed and turned to him, too fast for him to look away and pretend he hadn't been staring. 'It's beautiful,' she said after a moment's hesitation. 'The moon, I mean.'

'Yes,' he simply said, unable to shift his eyes from hers, knowing where the true beauty in this night lay.

Somewhere out in the desert an owl hooted. The fire crackled, spitting sparks into the air, and the moon hung low and fat in the sky, filled with expectation.

He could kiss her now under that moon. The air was ripe for it, the whole desert seemingly poised and waiting.

He had no right to make the desert wait.

She watched him draw nearer, shrinking the space between them until she could feel the heat emanating from him, feel the air shift with his approach. His breath was warm around her face, his dark eyes on her mouth, and she knew he was going to kiss her—and knew that there were one hundred good reasons why she shouldn't let him.

But for the life of her, with her senses buzzing and her skin alight, she couldn't remember a single one…

CHAPTER EIGHT

His lips tasted of sweet coffee and promises, of heated desire and the unmistakeable flavour of the man himself.

'It won't work,' she said in spite of the promise in his kiss, some shred of logic filtering through the fog of desire, that shred telling her that they been here before and it had not ended well that time.

He hushed her with his clever mouth and his persuasive lips and she let herself be persuaded for just a moment, giving herself up to his kiss and his touch, his hand at her throat feeling a frantic heartbeat in his touch, not knowing if it was his or hers.

The moment stretched and stretched. But she would stop this, she told herself, remembering another night when she had given herself up to his love-making, another night when she had given in to desire and passion only to be bluntly reminded of what he really thought of her. She remembered the anger she had felt then, trying to summon it up to give her strength when all she could feel was desire, need and the pulsing insistence between her thighs.

The low fire crackled and popped, somewhere close

by a camel softly snorted, and the indulgence of a moment became a minute or longer.

'Come to my tent,' he murmured, his hot mouth at her throat, his big hands molding her to him, his tongue writing its own scorching invitation on her flesh.

'No,' she whispered, turning her face away from his mouth, wishing she had been stronger from the start, wishing she was not so damned weak when it came to him despite all the hurt he had caused her, all the anger and despair. No, she revised—*because* of all the hurt, anger and despair. She should be stronger. 'I can't.'

But he didn't let her go. Instead his hand found one aching breast, brushing his thumb across her straining nipple, and she groaned into his mouth as spears of pleasure let fly to her core. 'Let's finish this, Marina. This time let's finish what we have started.'

With his hand making magic on her breast, and his hot mouth promising every conceivable pleasure, his words sounded so reasonable, so rational, that she almost succumbed.

But she had never wanted reasonable or rational from him. She had only ever wanted his love, in return for hers. And, in the end, that was what had killed their relationship.

She dragged in air, summoning all the strength she could find as she took his face between her hands and eased him away, a tear squeezing from her eye when she saw his eyes looked as tortured as she herself felt. 'Bahir,' she said, shaking her head slowly. 'Our time is past. It is gone. There is no point to this.'

Her words were met with an expression of disbelief, as if he could make no sense of her words. She smiled softly, trying to make him see. 'You know there is no point.' She watched his face as disbelief turned to disagreement and then anger. She waited and hoped that at least a flicker of understanding might follow, when he suddenly spun away from her and stood, clutching his head in his hands like it was set to explode and he needed to keep the two sides together.

'What do you want, Marina?'

She stood and straightened her *abaya*, smoothing out imaginary creases while she searched for an answer to his question. 'I want Chakir to know his father. Maybe even to have a good relationship with him.'

Chakir? He hadn't even been thinking about the boy. He'd been thinking about a woman who could turn him inside out with just one glance, who ran hot and cold in order to torment him.

'And us? What about us?'

She blinked back at him. 'If it is possible, I would like us to be friends.'

Friends!

She could look at him with those damned siren's eyes and that mouth—she could kiss him with that mouth—and yet tell him she wanted to be friends? How could they ever be merely friends? Couldn't she see that?

He looked up at the winking moon and wanted to howl out his anger, his frustration and his rumbling discontent. But instead he just sighed into the desert air. 'It's late,' he said, trying not to snarl, not entirely sure he was succeeding. 'I'll see you to your tent.'

He slept badly, a night of fractured nonsensical dreams filled with an unending and ultimately futile pursuit of something unseen that kept moving and shifting, something always just out of his reach.

Of course he would be frustrated, he rationalised the next morning as he hung over the sink and doused his head with cold water to clear the residual bleariness away. Twice now, she had worked him to fever pitch. Twice now she left him achingly hard with no release.

When had she grown this ability to say no, she who was once so eager for sex that she would not wear underwear in case it slowed them down? She who had never once said no to sex with him in all the time they'd been together, the one who had initiated it just as often as he had?

She thought that after all that, they could go from lovers to just friends? Who was she trying to kid?

Not him. Maybe she was trying to kid herself.

'The vehicles are packed,' Ahab said behind him from the door of the tent. 'Whenever you are ready, Bahir.'

He turned and thanked his old friend, already girding his loins for another day in *her* company. But maybe a day sightseeing in the Melted Gorge and showing his son the wonders of the region would distract him. Maybe a day trying to convince her she was kidding herself would distract him.

He looked at his face in the mirror as he towelled off the last of the water, trying hard not to notice the tiredness around his eyes. He could damned well do with a distraction.

But it wasn't the distraction he was looking for when he saw Marina sitting in the back seat with the children looking subdued and Catriona seated in the passenger seat alongside him. *Interesting,* he thought, climbing behind the wheel, feeling somewhat vindicated. So Marina was determined to stay out of his way? Maybe because she didn't think it was that simple to remain just friends either.

They set out in convoy across the desert floor along a wide flat road edged with random boulders hewn from the mountains around them, half a dozen vehicles filled with half the tribe, a holiday atmosphere prevailing as they set off to spend a day in the mountains.

If Marina was trying to hide from him, so be it. He focused on the excitement of his son, answering his eager questions about where they were going and what they would see. Even managing to answer the girl's one question when it came, without needing *her* prompt from the back seat, smiling to himself when he saw in the rear-vision mirror that she had noticed.

He could play the friends game, if that was what she wanted. He could tolerate a child she had made with someone else—that wasn't his—if it helped get Marina on side and convince her that being merely friends was nowhere near enough.

Onwards the convoy travelled across the stony desert, towards the mountains that loomed blue and imposing before them. They passed by a salt lake where storks rose in a black-and-white cloud that momentarily blotted out the morning sun. They passed by a pointy-eared desert fox standing sentry atop a sand dune, suspiciously monitoring their approach before they got too close and it turned and padded silently away.

He loved that his son got a kick out of these things,

and he got a kick out of seeing his excitement. It was almost like being a boy again himself, except…

No, not that, he thought, knowing he could not bear it if that happened to him. It was too late now to wish he would never have a child, but he would never wish what had happened to him on anyone, let alone a son of his.

She watched his eyes in the mirror, observing him from the back seat, silently applauding him when he explained something to Chakir, cheering him when he finally acknowledged a query from Hana, taking the time to answer. Hana had listened with her fingers in her mouth and with all the concentrated studiousness of a two-year-old. She, on the other hand, had listened with some kind of joy because for the first time she had not had to intercede on her daughter's behalf.

Instead, Bahir had answered her question as if it had been Chakir who had asked him. For that she was grateful and more than a little impressed. For a man who had never wanted children, he showed an interest in his son she would never have thought possible. For a man who had made a point of excluding Hana up until now, he seemed at least to be making an effort not to shunt her aside.

She wondered if Bahir had actually heard her last night, and understood her plea to be friends, and understood what that meant. She should not have stayed so late, getting wooed by the magical desert night, thinking that magic was meant for her. She should never have let him kiss her. But maybe her pleas had broken through some kind of barrier.

Maybe they could be friends after all.

It would not be like what they had shared before—there could be no return to those heady reckless times—but it would be something.

The gorge was tucked away like a secret, nothing to show it was there, the visitors disembarking to follow a trail that led towards a broad and winding cleft into the mountains. Excitement among the visitors was high. The children and adults were eager to enter the gorge—and not just for the picnic they knew they would enjoy afterwards—and it wasn't long before Marina could see why. The track narrowed as they progressed, winding and twisting its way through the rock, the walls either side growing higher.

And as they moved deeper into the cleft, the colours of the rock changed from sun-bleached white to a hundred shades, through honey and caramel and beyond, like someone had melted the rock and poured it back in swirling layers, while in other places crystalline colours of purples and vibrant greens sparkled from the walls.

'Wow,' said Chakir when Bahir had asked them to look up into a shaft where every colour they had already seen seemed to coalesce and merge in rippled layered poetry.

Hana just stopped behind her brother and stared upwards, her eyes wide, drinking it in, trying to make sense of it all. She pulled her fingers from her mouth to reveal a wide smile. 'Pretty,' she said.

She saw Bahir's eyes on Hana, a small frown hovering at the bridge of his nose, before he turned his gaze to her and the frown slipped away. He cocked one eyebrow, as if waiting for her reaction, and she had to resist the urge to think he had brought them to the place purely for her benefit and hers alone. She smiled. 'It's amazing.'

But it was the smile he sent right back at her that zapped up her spine and lit all the places that had ached with want last night. And she shivered with the unwanted pleasure of it, wondering if there would ever come a time when he did not make her sizzle with just one look.

Had she been kidding herself last night with him? Would she ever be satisfied with merely being friends with a man who she knew could blow her world apart with one touch of his clever fingers or one swipe of his wicked tongue?

She swallowed down on a pang of fruitless longing. But they had proved it would not work any other way. She wasn't that reckless good-time girl any more. She could no longer afford to be. And he seemed to be filled with a hatred for something that almost consumed him.

They both had changed in the intervening years. They were both different people, but they were both also Chakir's parents. So for their son's sake, then, it would have to be friendship and they would just have to try to make it work.

The group emerged both awe-struck and panting from the climb out of the gorge to a picnic lunch set in the shadow of the cliff, Chakir and Hana took no more time than it took to grab the first thing they could off a tray before running off to play with their new-found friends.

'They'll be okay?' Marina asked, taking a few steps

after them as her two trailed after the others, itching to follow herself just in case.

She sensed him at her shoulder. 'They'll be fine.'

She took a deep breath and forced her feet to stay where they were, but it was so, so hard to see Hana running so wild and free when she had promised to take good care of her. At home in Tuscany, she knew the local hazards. It was another thing here, in the desert, where everything was so new to them and so unfamiliar. Even when they had visited her father's home in Jemeya, they'd been there for such a short time that there'd hardly been time to venture outside the palace walls, let alone run around in the desert.

'But there are dangers in the desert.'

'As you say, princess,' he said. 'In the desert, there are always dangers lurking.'

His words had her looking at him, looking into his dark eyes, wondering at his meaning and wishing for things that she knew she should not. Knowing he was right. For the dangers of the desert were everywhere.

And right now Bahir was the most dangerous thing of all.

She turned away, shivering, her eyes following the children running and wheeling in circles, their arms outstretched like that flock of cranes they'd seen earlier today. Hana—tiny, precious Hana—lagged behind them all, flapping her arms and making her smile. 'And that's supposed to make me feel more comfortable, is it?'

She heard his sigh beside her. 'Maybe you could cut her some slack.'

'What? Cut who some slack?'

'The girl,' he said, adding, 'Hana,' before she could

correct him. 'You act like she's made of glass or some-thing, always hovering over her. Why don't you let her just be a child?'

'You don't understand,' she said, shaking her head. 'Hana's special.'

He grunted. 'I can see that.'

She glared at him. 'You just don't like her. Full stop.'

'Why should I? I didn't ask you to bring her. She's not my child.'

'And that's all that matters is it? The only people who count are those fathered by your fertile loins?'

'What do you expect me to say? I never wanted a child. That you present me with one was enough to deal with, without his sister coming along for the ride.' He looked over at her and shrugged. 'But she's all right. Kind of cute, in a way.'

Her head swung around. He'd actually noticed some-thing about Hana besides the fact she wasn't his? Maybe that question of hers he'd answered in the car hadn't been an aberration. Maybe his stance was softening to-wards the tiny girl. 'She's beautiful,' she said, thinking of Sarah, seeing her mother's pixie face every time she looked at the daughter. Hana was a miniature Sarah. Even her laugh reminded her of her friend.

'Not that she looks a lot like you.'

Danger shimmied down her spine, electric and spark-ing, chasing away any feelings of well-being and put-ting her senses on red alert. Somehow she managed a shrug, feigning indifference, while her self-protection systems registered the need to close this conversation down and now.

There was one sure way. 'Perhaps,' she said, already

turning back towards the safety of the group, 'that's because she looks more like her father.'

Who was he? he wanted to ask as he watched her go, both dissatisfied with her answer and disgruntled that she could so boldly walk away, her back so stiff and straight, her jaw set high, as if she was claiming some kind of moral high-ground. Who was this wonderful man that his daughter was so special? Where was he now and what was he doing? Was he busy with a wife while he put Marina up in his mountain retreat and let her look after his child?

Whoever he was, one thing was certain: his child would never live in another man's house, no matter who Hana's father was.

He watched her return to the picnic, to a group of women including Catriona where they exchanged words and both glanced over to where the children had been playing before. He followed their gaze to see them all now squatting in a circle, one of the older boys making pictures in the sand with a stick. He would be telling them a story, Bahir knew. He could almost hear drifts of the boy's unbroken voice on the still air.

He remembered sitting in such a circle himself, listening to his cousin telling a story about the first Bedouins and how they had conjured up a camel in their dreams, a soft-footed beast that would carry them safely across the shifting desert sands, and how they had been woken by a terrifying noise only to find the first camels bellowing outside their tents, impatient to be put to work.

He saw his son listen, open-mouthed in wonder. He heard his laughter, and that terrible weight inside him shifted unexpectedly again, jamming up tight against his lungs so he could barely breathe.

The wind lifted and he heard it almost sigh as it swirled past in a rustle of sand and the whispered voices of his brothers, of his mother and his father, of all the people of the tribe calling to him.

He put his hands to his head and spun around, his feet taking him further away, away from the chatter of women and the low murmurings of the men; away from the laughter of children. But the one sound he really wanted to blank out was the sound of the ghosts of the past.

Didn't they understand?

He wasn't ready to face them yet.

Marina watched him go, sensing his pain in every tortured step. 'Will he be all right, do you think?' she asked as Ahab joined them. 'Do you think someone should go with him?'

The old man watched through sun-creased eyes. 'Some things a man can only do by himself.'

She looked at him, wondering at his answer, wondering at the things he was not telling her before she looked back at the retreating form of Bahir in the distance. 'But he's hurting.'

'The hurt he is feeling was inflicted a long time ago. Perhaps he is only now starting to feel the pain.'

'What hurt? What happened to him? Is it something to do with his family?'

'Bahir will tell you,' the old man said, with a nod of his sage head. 'In his own time.'

* * *

He wandered aimlessly, retracing his steps and finding himself back in the gorge, where the coloured walls rose high above him, ancient and full of the wisdom of the world. A wisdom that eluded him, a wisdom he had no clue to understand, until a mournful wind sang through the gorge and drove him away. He then found himself back near the picnic under the cliffs, knowing he was walking in senseless circles and not understanding, but simply driven to walk.

Until it occurred to him that his life was on the same aimless course.

That she was right.

Because, when it all came down to it, what did he actually do? He gambled. What did he produce? Nothing. Not really. Of course, it was easy to think he was producing something when he was winning. He was making money. He had stacks of chips to show for it, he had investments salted away with whatever proceeds exceeded his immediate expenses, and there were plenty of those, because he was good at what he did. But, beyond that, what did he do? What good was he to anyone?

God, he thought, suddenly sick of the soul-searching, sick of it all. He had planned to come to the desert to lift his spirits, not to find fault with himself. So what that he didn't own a home? He didn't need one. So why must he beat himself up about things he could not change and did not need changing?

He was good at what he did. He was the best. When it came to playing the roulette wheel, nobody risked so much or won so much. Wasn't that some kind of achievement in itself?

A cry rang out in the desert air—a child's cry. He'd

half-turned towards the sound, taking in the picture around him, registering a scattering of children across the sands wandering tired and thirsty back to the picnic, when he heard Marina's cry.

'Hana?' she called, half-question in her voice, half-fear, just before the girl's scream came again, shrill and panicked and slicing through the desert air like a sharpened blade. And this time he found the source. The girl was screaming from where she'd fallen on the rocky ground, her tiny limbs rigid. For a split second he assumed she must have hurt herself falling while trying to keep up with the others, and he waited for her to pick herself up off the ground, until he noticed her attention focused on the ugly black shape marching menacingly towards her across the sand.

CHAPTER NINE

'HANA!' he roared, already launching himself towards her. 'Hana, get up. Move!'

But the child was petrified with fear as the arachnid marched purposefully on, its tail curved over its head, poised and ready to inflict its sting.

The air erupted with cries of panic and warning as everyone suddenly realised what was happening. His lungs heaving, Bahir sprinted the distance between them, barely registering others charging for the scene, aware only that there was movement. His eyes were on the girl.

'Mama!' she squealed between sobs, pushing herself backwards across the sand on her hands, her eyes fixed on the approaching terror.

Why didn't she run? She had to run. She was much too small to survive a sting from a scorpion and he would never get there in time. All of these thoughts ran through his head in the seconds it took him to reach her, seconds that stretched and bulged with impossibility as he dived in one desperate lunge and plucked her from the path of danger, rolling away across the desert floor.

For a moment the girl in his arms was too shocked to make a sound, but as he stood she recovered enough to scream again, louder this time if it were possible, howling her protest and twisting her body away, wanting desperately to be free.

And, even though one of the men wielded a stick and flicked the scorpion away, he would not let her go while that thing was anywhere near.

'Hana!' Marina cried, her feet flying across the sand towards them, her robe flapping hard against her legs, and he saw her beautiful face drained of so much colour that she could have been made of the desert sands.

The girl held out her arms to her and, breathless, Marina took the child and clutched her to her chest, pressing her lips to her curls as she sobbed helplessly against her shoulder. 'Oh God, Hana,' she said as her sobs quietened. 'It's okay. You're all right now.'

She looked at Bahir through tear-filled eyes, her voice still shaky. 'I tried not to panic. I thought about what you said and I forced myself not to run to Hana straightaway and pick her up like I usually do. And then I saw it moving on the sand next to her.' She shuddered, rocking the child in her arms. 'If you hadn't got there in time…'

He cursed himself for his ill-timed advice. 'I should never have said anything to you. If I'd thought it was as serious, I would have been there sooner.'

Eyes a man could drown in blinked up at him. 'Thank you.'

He dusted himself off to give his hands something to do other than to pull her trembling form into his arms, child and all, and comfort her. 'You might want to check her for scratches,' he said. 'I tried to keep her off the ground, but she might have got a scrape or two.'

Chakir caught up with them, his eyes bright with excitement. 'Can you teach me how to do that?' he asked, and Bahir almost found it in himself to laugh.

'Maybe later,' he said, thinking that they'd had enough excitement for one day. Besides, there was something he had to do, something he could not put off any longer, the voices in his head became louder and more insistent. But first he had to get this lot home. 'I think right now we should head back to the camp, don't you?'

The journey home was a quiet one, both the children asleep within five minutes of setting off, exhausted after the day's activities, Catriona sleepily staring out of her window and dozing off long before they reached the camp.

This time Marina sat in the front seat alongside him, watching his long-fingered hands on the wheel, looking relaxed and confident, feeling anything but relaxed and confident herself as she tried to make sense of the man alongside her—a man who cared nothing for a child and yet had risked his own life to protect hers. For she was under no misapprehension as to the enormity of his actions. A scorpion sting could threaten the life of a grown man, shutting down his respiratory system, closing his throat and paralysing his lungs. A child Hana's size wouldn't stand a chance, not out here so far from medical assistance.

She glanced behind her, saw that they were all asleep and said softly to him, 'You saved her life today, you know.'

He shrugged, as if it was nothing; as if it was something he did every day. 'I was the closest to her, that's all.'

'Maybe. And I know I thanked you back there,' she said, 'but I'm not sure it was anywhere near enough. Thank you for doing what you did and reaching Hana in time.'

He glanced across at her. 'I would have done the same for any child in danger.'

'I know, it's just that I know you're not that interested in Hana. Whereas Chakir, on the other hand...'

He swung his head around, a scowl tugging at his brows. 'You think I would save my own son and yet leave another's child to suffer a terrible fate?'

'No.' She shook her head, knowing that had come out wrong. 'That wasn't what I meant. I was just surprised that you were the one to act when it wasn't your child in danger, and when you had made such a point in the past about her not being your child.'

He shook his head and looked back at the road. 'So maybe at the time that didn't seem the most pertinent detail.' And she felt his rebuke in his words as he drew a thick black line under the conversation before she'd had a chance to say the things she really wanted to say.

The things she should say.

For in Bahir rescuing Hana, she'd been reminded of her own rescue from the twisted Mustafa, who'd kidnapped her sister, Aisha, to claim the throne of Al-Jirad for his own. And then, when that purpose was foiled, kidnapped her to frustrate his half-brother Zoltan's ascension to the thrown. She'd tried to downplay Bahir's role in her rescue, tried to make out he was only there because his three friends, Zoltan, Kabar and Rashid, expected it—and maybe that had been one element of it—but he had still been one of their party. He had still been there to ensure her safe return to her family.

And now he had rescued her again, for in saving Hana he had saved the promise she had made to the dying Sarah.

She sighed. 'I'm sorry. Now I've gone and offended you. What I was actually trying to lead up to, though so clumsily I'll admit, was to thank you, and properly this time, for your part in my rescue from Mustafa. I don't think I've ever done that. I'm only sorry now that it's so overdue.'

The last thing she expected in return for her thanks was a smile. His features were in profile as his eyes remained on the road, scanning the wide sandy route ahead, but she definitely saw his lips turn up, his cheek creasing along a rarely seen line.

'What? You're actually thanking me, princess, while all time I was out there I was merely having fun with my friends? What was it you called us—a band of merry men out on some boys' own adventure?'

She slumped back in her seat, mortified. God, had she really said that? It was a miracle he'd bothered trying to save Hana at all, ungrateful as she had been for his part in her rescue. 'You have to forgive me.' She searched for even more words to apologise, searched for the right words, and in the end could only come up with a poor excuse. 'I was angry with you at the time.'

'It's all right,' he said, sounding as though it was anything but, looking over at her then with eyes so devoid of life that she wondered what he was thinking that could have put that look there. 'I know all about anger.'

His words made her shiver, weighted down with

some kind of pain. She didn't ask what he meant as the camp came into view. She wasn't sure she wanted to know. Once before she'd been on the receiving end of his anger and she knew enough not to want to go back there ever again.

She remembered that day now as she watched the desert slide past her window, when he had blown apart her world with the force of his anger and cast her out of his life for ever.

At least, it had been meant to be for ever. Yet here they were, forced together again by circumstances, by the existence of their son Chakir.

Sometimes the anger was still there. It was only too clear, simmering away under the surface, only too willing to bubble up and break free. But at other times it was another emotion, just as heated and potent, that seemed to drive his actions.

And she wondered how she could ever have had a relationship with him for all those months, all those nights, without realising the mystery within the man, those different parts of him, or asking all the questions she had now about who he truly was.

The vehicle neared the camp site, a traditional Bedouin camp complete with opulent tents for their guests, and that raised still more questions in her mind. He'd made the decision to bring Chakir to the desert and, lo, all this had been laid on in honour of their visitors.

'How did you organise all this?'

'You mean the picnic?'

'No. I mean us, here, in the middle of a desert where you haven't lived for years apparently. And one day you

decide we will all go to the desert and the next there is
an entire encampment set up and waiting for us. How
is that even possible?'

He shrugged. 'Cash speaks loudly out here where
they have little chance to earn it.'

'But so quickly? One moment you decide to go to
the desert and the next there is this waiting for you?'

'Not really. I was planning to come anyway after
taking you home, so I'd already made a few calls and
chased up some contacts. Finding Ahab alive made it
easy. When I told him there were more coming with me,
he knew where to find the tents I needed. He suggested
staying with his tribe—one of the last to resist urban-
isation and live as traditionally as possible—instead of
camping alone as I'd originally intended.'

'I like it,' she said, thinking of the new friends they
had already made and the adventures they had enjoyed,
despite the traumas of today. 'The tribespeople are so
welcoming, to all of us.'

'It's the Bedouin way,' he said with an unexpected
note of pride. Unexpected, because he had not thought
of himself as Bedouin for years, his lifestyle so removed
from that culture. 'Visitors are honoured guests. I had
not thought there were any tribes still living in such a
simple manner. So much of the world has moved on.'

Hadn't he himself moved on?

'But your people lived this way.'

A pause. And, even though he was sitting behind
the wheel of a car driving along a desert road, still it
felt like the sand had shifted under his feet like that
first step into quicksand when the world tilted and went
wrong. 'Mostly.'

'And this is how you grew up—herding goats, sitting around camp fires listening to stories at night, watching the stars and your father teaching you to swim?'

He felt the weight of the years bearing down on him, the oppressive weight of dusty memories. 'A million years ago,' he said, through a throat clogged with the sands of time.

'So where is your tribe now?' she asked as they drove into the camp at the head of the snaking convoy. 'Where is your family? I asked Ahab and he said you would tell me.'

He braked the car to a halt, and sat there while the passengers in the back seat roused and blinked into wakefulness, looking as bewildered as he felt, but knowing the time had come.

All afternoon he'd felt it. All afternoon his duty had called to him. And what better way to explain it to her, if she was so damned curious and when words seemed so thin on the barren ground?

He undid his seatbelt, put one hand to his door handle and looked at her. 'I'm going to visit them after we've unpacked. Maybe you should join me. Maybe then you might understand.'

Should she? There was a power of unspoken meaning in his invitation, along with a measure of challenge in his eyes. But what did it mean? For a while she'd wondered the worst, that he had been hiding some dreadful truth from her about his family. Equally, she had wondered if they had disowned him after he had turned to a life of gambling in the casinos of the world.

But now he talked of visiting them…

Had they now agreed to see him, knowing he was back? Had they heard word via Ahab of their grandson?

'And Chakir?'

'No. Not the boy. It's too soon.'

Relief washed through her. They had not yet told Chakir that Bahir was his father, not even sure he would understand, and for the moment that was how she wanted it to stay. Maybe she was being over-cautious, but she wanted to wait at least until she knew that Bahir wanted to be a permanent part of his son's life. She did not want to have to explain where his father had gone, if he suddenly changed his mind and opted out of Chakir's life.

'Don't worry,' he said, taking her reticence for reluctance. 'It was probably a bad idea.'

'No,' she said. 'I'll come.'

It was a bad idea, he realised as they headed away from the camp and towards a range of craggy blue hills in the distance along little more than a stony track. An exceptionally bad idea to have her along.

But at least she'd stopped asking questions. She was sitting silent alongside him as the vehicle lurched its way forward. Soon enough she would have all the answers she needed and more. Not that it might make any difference, but at least she would be closer to understanding why he had said what he had that day.

And, if she understood, maybe one day she could forgive him. But then he remembered her stricken face and the unshed tears in her eyes—the hurt and desolation—and he would not be surprised if she never forgave him for so completely destroying what they once had.

But she would know the truth of his family.

They scaled one of the ridges rising from the valley and the pounding in his blood grew louder, more urgent, sending heat pulsing around his body until his skin felt almost blistering, sweat broke out on his forehead, marked his armpits and stuck his back to the seat.

One more ridge. It had been years since he had been here and he'd been little more than a child. Just that one time and so long ago, and still he remembered the jagged line of mountain against the sky, still he knew exactly where he was going.

But it was more than memory directing him, for it was almost as if he could feel their hands on the wheel, their collective wisdom guiding the vehicle along the stony track.

Guiding him home.

Home. If that wasn't a strange concept already for a Bedouin, where no fixed address was a way of life and the entire desert was your back yard. So your family and your tribe were your home. How much stranger for him, where his family was gathered in a place of the dead.

And yet still they called to him.

What would he tell them?

What could he possibly say that they would want to hear?

The four-wheel drive ground up the stony incline, the heat in his veins building with it, the weight in his gut lurching with every kick of the steering wheel in his hands.

Just shy of the crest, he stopped and pulled the handbrake on.

'Why are we stopping here?' she asked uncertainly,

looking around, searching for answers. 'What is this place?'

Looking around would tell her nothing, he knew. There was nothing to see but sand, rocky ground and the occasional saltbush, but now they were here he could not find the words to tell her. Soon, he knew she would work it out for herself. But now that they were there, he could not do this with her along. Not yet. First he needed time to make his peace and to collect himself again. 'Wait here,' he instructed, without explaining, leaving the engine on and the air-conditioning running. 'I won't be long.'

Before waiting for her answer, he climbed out into the hot, dry air, pushing the door firmly closed with both hands, his gaze on the track to where it disappeared over the rise, already anticipating the scene that awaited him.

Then with a deep breath he pushed purposefully away from the car and, with a weight in his heart so heavy it was a wonder it didn't fall through his chest, he set off up the track.

He stopped when he reached the crest and looked down into the shallow valley where once a few low black tents had clustered around a tiny oasis, around which a dozen kids had chased each other, laughing and full of life.

Once so full of life.

Where now there was nothing but an eerie wind that coaxed the desert sand into a mournful dance around a few ragged lines of flat white stones set into the rocky earth.

His family.

The wind circled him as he walked closer, imprisoning him, celebrating his capture as it whipped around the stones, presenting him like a prize.

He stood at the base of one of the twenty-six simple stones, now worn ragged with the ravages of the elements, overcome by the enormity of what had happened here.

Overcome with the guilt that there should have been one more flat white stone.

He fell to his knees on the sandy ground and put one hand to the stone, warm under his touch like the living once had been.

'Father,' he said as the first of his tears soaked into the thirsty ground. 'I'm back. I've come home.'

How long was not long in the desert? Bahir had been gone the best part of thirty minutes and still there was no sign of him. A gnawing worry in Marina's gut refused to be ignored any longer.

Why had he not returned? What was taking him so long?

He'd walked up that track and then stood there, looking down at something, and everything about his stance had suggested he was a man defeated.

And then he'd disappeared behind the ridge and she had been left wondering. But from the ridge top she might be able to see.

She leaned over the driver's side and turned off the ignition, slipping from the car into air so dry the moisture was as good as sucked from her lungs. A breeze found her then, playing a haunting tune as it toyed with the ends of her hair, plucking at the hem of her light *abaya* as she headed up the track.

A sad place, she thought, shivering with the premonition, for even though it was as starkly beautiful as any other places she had seen in Jaqbar, there was emptiness mixed with sorrow on the wind, turning the desert desolate.

Then she reached the crest of the hill and saw him a little way away, kneeling on the sand, and for a moment she felt relief that she had found him—until she noticed the flat white stones poking from the earth all around him, and the sad wind moaned its mournful song as her heart squeezed tight. 'Oh no, Bahir,' she whispered, knowing it was as bad as it could possibly be, and still wishing it not to be true. 'Please not that.'

Scant minutes later, she knelt by his side before one of the simple stones, not looking at him, giving him time to register her presence. Only after she was certain he had was she willing to ask, 'Who are they?'

'My family,' he said, his voice sounding strained and choked. 'Let me introduce you to them. He pointed at a stone alongside. 'There is my mother.' He pointed to the next. 'My father.' He listed them as he went. 'My cousins, my uncles, my aunt, her mother. They are all here.'

'And who is this one?'

'This one—this is my baby brother, Jemila. He was three. The same age as Chakir is now.' His voice broke on their child's name. She looked at his face for the first time and saw the tracks of his tears down his cheeks and her heart broke.

'Oh, Bahir.'

'There are twenty-six in all,' he said matter-of-factly

without returning her gaze. 'An entire tribe. All except for one.'

'All except you.'

'I was at school in England,' he said blankly. 'The pride of the family. The chosen one. The one upon whom all the hopes and dreams of the tribe resided.' He shook his head. 'I was twelve years old when I learned a traveller had been found ill in the desert and brought to the camp to be revived. But he died, and one by one, they all fell sick—the old, the young, the strong. The disease made no exception. It wasn't until two weeks after they had been buried that they finally tracked me down to let me know.'

'Bahir,' she uttered softly, not knowing what she could possibly say that might comfort him, instead simply wrapping an arm around his shoulders just to let him know she was there, surprised he felt cold under her hand when the day was so warm. 'I'm so sorry.'

He lifted his face to the heavens then, his features tight and etched with grief. 'I was supposed to be here. It was term break and I had always come home for holidays. Except this time I had an invitation to go home with a classmate. I had never had a Christmas before and I saw the excitement of the other boarders, all looking forward to going home to parties and to presents, and I knew my parents would insist I came home. So I told them that I was held back by the masters, to catch up on my studies. I told her I could not come home.'

He sagged, dropping his head almost to the ground. 'I lied to my father and my mother. I should have been here with them. I should be here now, buried under one of these stones. I should have been here with them.'

Finally she understood the full horror of his past; finally she realised the agony and the pain that had shaped him and made him the man he was, the man racked with survivor guilt. She squeezed his shoulders, trying to lend him her warmth and chase away the chill of the past that possessed him. 'They would have wanted you to survive. They would not blame you. Nobody would blame you.'

'I don't need anyone else to blame me. Don't you think I have blame enough? I lied to my family. I was not here when I should have been, and for my sins I would have to live with that for ever.'

'Bahir, you must not blame yourself.'

'Who else is to blame? Who else is left to blame?' He dragged in air, and she could hear the agony that consumed him and bent him double.

'I swore that day, the day they brought me to this place, that I would sooner never have a child than risk leaving him with nobody and nothing. Nothing but guilt.'

Beside him she ached with the pain that seemed to ooze from his pores. 'You never wanted a child because you never wanted him to suffer as you did. As you still do.'

He shook his head violently from side to side. 'No!' he roared, putting his hands to his forehead before rising, anguished, to his feet, staggering away from the simple graveyard towards a cluster of palms where the sunlight filtered through the leaves and where a tiny spring kept alive a thin border of grass. She followed at a distance, feeling helpless and heartsick, not knowing what to say or do, knowing only that her own heart was breaking as she watched him fall to his knees, dip his hands into the pool and splash water on his face. He rocked back on his heels, his eyes empty, focused on nothing but the past.

'They're the ones who suffered. Not me. I lived through it all. I went home with my friend and laughed and played games and had no idea what was happening out here in the desert.

'And then, in one fell swoop, I had nothing. I had nobody. I should have been with them!' he cried. 'I wish I had been here!'

He squeezed his eyes tightly shut, his face screwed up tight, and she saw the tears squeezing from his eyes as his grief overwhelmed him.

There was not one thing on earth she could say, not one thing she could do, other than to kneel down alongside, hold him, press her mouth to his salty tears and kiss them away.

He sagged against her. He let her hold his head in her hands. He let her kiss his tortured face and stroke her hands through his hair as she nestled his head against her chest. He let her comfort him as the sobs racked his body and his anguished cries rang out across the desert, as the warm breeze wrapped itself around them and held them in its whispering embrace.

Until the wind shifted subtly to a caress and comfort turned to need, and he was kissing her too, his mouth seeking hers. It was done tentatively at first—so hesitant, unsure and so very pained—and then hungrily, like a man starved and falling upon his first meal in days. It was all she could do to keep up with the demands of his urgent mouth and his hot, seeking hands.

She made no move to stop him. She would not stop him. He had lost so very much and all she had to offer him was the comfort of her body in the life-affirming act of sex.

He set her down softly on the grass, his kisses filled with a hungry desperation that wrenched at her soul and made her want to weep for him, to weep for the boy he had been, the boy who felt he had betrayed his family, the boy who had lost everything without the hint of a goodbye. So she put her heart into her kiss, wanting to make up for his sorrow, wanting to take away his pain for ever. Wanting to lend him hope.

He took everything she could give, wanting more. She felt his hand skim down her side, felt the slide of her *abaya* up her legs, and she shifted to enable him to slip it over her hips. She let him tug it over her shoulders, gazing down at her with broken eyes filled with ghosts and a savage, desperate need.

And, while he watched, she slipped off her bra and underwear and lay back on the grassy bank, offering herself to him.

With a groan etched in pain he tore at his shirt and his pants and in a blur of white linen, bunched muscles and golden skin he was back at her mouth, frantic now, his skin against her skin, his hardness pressing into her belly, his legs finding a home between hers.

She arched beneath him, her breath hitched as he found her pulsing core, aching now with her own escalating need, aching for completion. She moaned with the very closeness of it, with the absence and with the promise, forgetting for a moment that this was about pleasuring him.

'Bahir,' she whispered, the sound of his name laced with desperation.

He answered with a growl and a thrust of his hips that drove his hard length into her, filling her so deliciously, so exquisitely that it forced tears from her eyes.

It had always been good with Bahir, she remembered as he remained buried deep inside her. He had always been the best. But surely she would have remembered if holding him deep within her body had been this good?

Then he drew back and all that was good became better in the slide of flesh against flesh and the anticipation of his return. He captured a peaked nipple between his lips, drawing it into his mouth as he drove into her again, and sparks went off behind her eyes. His mouth captured the other breast in time for his next powerful lunge.

All of a sudden there was no time for niceties, no time to cosset. There was only time to cling onto him as she felt her peak building exponentially with every fluid thrust of his hips, every quickening stroke.

Until she could take no more and she shattered around him in a blaze of stars. From another galaxy it seemed she heard his cry, triumph in the desperation, victory in his anguish, and she reached for him as he too reached the stars, holding him close, comforting him as she guided him safely back to earth.

Loving him.

For, even though she knew she could never tell him, she knew in her heart that she loved Bahir. She had never stopped loving him.

They lay there in the dappled shade as day slipped

away and the slanting sun turned the desert into a sea of gold.

'I never cried for them,' he told her, holding her tucked up against him, stroking her hair. 'I couldn't. I was too ashamed. I was too angry.'

'It's okay,' she said, wanting to weep for a boy who hadn't been able to bring himself to cry.

'No.' He sighed, taking his hand from her hair, dropping the back of his wrist on his forehead. 'It's not okay. That day you came, when I got angry…'

'Hush,' she said, with a finger to his lips. 'It doesn't matter. I understand.'

He grabbed her hand, curled it in his long fingers and pressed it to his lips. 'No. There is more. After my family died, the college agreed to extend my scholarship. There was no point, they said, in sending me home. There was nothing for me there. And so a foster family was found for me, an Arab man working in London in corporate finance who claimed to be some distant relative. A cruel man. A man with a simpering excuse for a wife, a man who would beat me with a cane if I didn't top every class, every exam. A man who thought he was grooming me for a career alongside him. I hated him.'

He shook his head. 'I knew I had to get away but I needed money. That's when I started gambling. That's when I realised I had a gift for it. He beat me more when he found out what I was doing and that only made me more determined. By the time I was sixteen, I had made enough that I never had to go back there again.

'That day you came over—that very morning—I had woken to the voices of my family in my head. I had dreamed of them that night, I had dreamed of the day twenty years before when I had stood here and been presented with the truth, that my family and everyone I loved, my whole world, had been taken from me.'

'No wonder you were upset that day.'

'But that wasn't it. It was a package from a lawyer that came that morning—it contained a letter telling me my foster father had died. And it contained my father's ring, a necklace of my mother and the amulet that had been around Jemila's neck when he had died. My family's things. My foster father had kept them all those years. He had never so much as told me they existed.

'And I was so angry—with my foster father, yes, but with my family for leaving me to such a fate. And with myself, for lying and partying with a friend when I should have been with them. On that day, I hated them all and I hated myself, and then you walked in talking family.' He shook his head. 'I savaged you because you stumbled into my nightmare talking about things I never wanted any part of that day more than ever.'

He dragged in a chestful of air and let it go, as if letting the weight of the past go with it. She realised the full horror of her own blundering actions, that she had chosen that day of all days to declare her love and share the excitement of the child they had unwittingly made together. She raised herself up on her elbow and leaned over him. 'I'm so sorry. I didn't know. I had no idea.'

'How could you, when I had never spoken of these things, when I had buried the past under an anger so deep it could never resurface? But that day there was no forgetting any of it.'

She shook her head. She could not imagine.

'To think, I was the chosen one,' he said, bitterness

infusing his words. 'I was the great hope of the tribe, born with a gift for numbers and so sent off to school in England—a rare privilege for my people, one they hoped would bring the tribe great benefits and wealth. They were all so proud of me—my father, my mother...'

He shook his head and turned away. 'And look how I have repaid them—by becoming a gambler. A wastrel. And, even though I finished school and paid for university with my winnings, what point was a degree when I turned straight to the university of spin? What point has been this life that was saved when all others were lost? What good have I ever done for them?'

'What could you possibly do?' she said, stroking the thick hair behind his ear, making circles with her fingertips at his pulsing temple. 'Nothing would bring them back. What could you do?'

'I should have done something! You'd think I would have achieved something other than notoriety in every gambling den in the world.'

'But you had lost everything.'

She splayed her fingers though his thick hair, winding her fingers around its strong waves. 'And maybe that's why you gamble,' she mused, wondering out loud, trying to fit the tortured pieces together. 'Because money is not like people. Money can be won and lost and then won again, and the pain of losing it, if any, is transitory. Maybe because, ultimately, there is no real risk.'

He turned his head back to her, a frown at the bridge of his nose as though he didn't understand, and she wondered if she'd been speaking a foreign language.

'I never wanted a child,' he said. 'I never wanted family.'

'I know. I understand.'

'But I want Chakir. I want my son.'

She nodded, her chest too tight to speak.

Then he pulled her to him. 'And I want his mother too.'

CHAPTER TEN

'MARRY me,' he said in the next breath, before she'd had a chance to absorb his previous declaration. Before the beat of her heart had had a chance to settle.

'Bahir, I—'

'It makes sense, don't you see? Chakir needs a father. I never wanted a family, it's true, but I can't turn my back on what's happened. And my father would be so proud to have a grandson and to see that I have done something good with my life.'

'But marriage?'

'I don't want to be a part-time father. I want to be there for him every day. And I swear I will try to be a good father to him. Besides, we're good together, Marina, you know we are. We can make it work for Chakir's sake.'

For Chakir's sake.

How ironic. 'Chakir's sake' was the very reason she'd decided to tell Bahir about their son's existence in the first place, and now he was using it to convince her to marry him.

Was it reason enough?

Maybe it made sense for Chakir, but what about Hana? Wanting to take on Chakir was one thing, but had he even thought about what getting married would entail? That he would have to be a father to Hana too?

And what about love? Was there no place for love in this arrangement? Had he lost the ability to love when he'd lost his entire family?

'I don't know,' she said, conflicted and floundering in uncertainty, only half-aware of the heated stroke of his hand down her body, lingering at her hip, his long fingers splayed over sensitive skin. 'It's too big a decision. I need time to think. And you need time to decide that's what you really want.'

'You're right,' he said, pulling her head down to his to brush his lips against her mouth. 'I could use the time. To persuade you.'

They made love again as the golden desert turned to silver under the rising moon and the desert wind felt like the whisper of silk over their skin. Their love-making was slower this time, Bahir taking his time to taste, explore and revisit; taking his own sweet time to persuade, so that when they joined again, their bodies and senses were at fever pitch and release slammed through her like a thunderbolt in a desert storm. She lay there in the aftermath, her breathing ragged, her body humming, and knew that she was no closer to making a decision.

But there was one thing she knew: that persuasion had never felt so good.

It was only when they were on their way back to the camp, when she felt the warm trickle of his juices in her underwear, that she realised that neither of them had given a moment's thought to protection.

She turned to him, stricken, wondering how either of them could have been so thoughtless—so *irrespon-*

sible—half-wondering if this had been part of Bahir's plan to force her hand. But no, she thought, thinking of the graveyard and Bahir's intense grief, there had been no planned seduction. It had been an oversight, that was all. A foolish one but maybe one without consequences, she thought, rolling over the dates of the calendar in her head. It was late in her cycle. The chances would be slim. Surely fate would not deal her such a hand again...?

Bahir was not slow in backing up his words with action. He proved over the next few days that he would make an excellent father for Chakir. He showed him how to read the footprints on the sand, to tell a camel from a horse, a fox from a wild goat. She watched him teach their son things he would never have learned otherwise.

Even with tiny Hana he showed an interest as she trailed around after him and Chakir, wanting to be included in everything. She wondered and hoped that his resentment of Hana was waning, and that his rescue of her from the scorpion had established some kind of bond between them.

But Bahir saved his most persuasive arguments for their love-making. He was nothing if not resourceful, finding reasons for them to be alone so that he could work his potent brand of persuasion on her. Unlike that reckless evening in the desert, though, when neither had given a thought to protection, he took every care.

Every time they met he asked her if she had made up her mind, if she was closer to deciding.

And every time she shook her head and asked for him to be patient. There was no hurry, she told herself, waiting for him to give her the one thing she craved, to say those tiny words she so longed to hear.

She wasn't brave enough to say them to him—the words he had once flung in shreds back in her face.

In the end, it wasn't the sex that made her decide, or anything he said. It wasn't even watching him with their adoring son, or lifting Hana onto a foal and showing her how to hold onto the reins when her tiny feet dangled way above the stirrups.

It was the new well he paid for and helped build, bare-backed and sweating, slogging it out on the rocky ground alongside the men from the tribe.

It was the books he ordered and had delivered so the children of the camp could learn to read and write at home and not be forced to go to school in Souza, far away from their families.

It was all the changes she witnessed in him that made up her mind.

This was a different man from the one she'd known and partied with all those years ago. This man seemed to have found purpose in his life, even taking to wearing the robes of his people when he was amongst them.

This man had discovered how to laugh and live and maybe, hopefully, how to love.

And she wanted to spend the rest of her life with him.

'He's asked me to marry him,' she confided to Catriona that night as they prepared the children for bed, before she was due to meet him. He'd planned a surprise, he'd told her, 'something special', and her senses were buzzing in anticipation.

The older woman smiled and hugged her. 'I knew

something must be happening because of the stars in your eyes lately. Have you said yes?'

'I'm planning to tonight. Except it means leaving the children with you for a few hours, if that's all right. Bahir has something special planned, apparently.'

Catriona squeezed her hand. 'Of course you can leave them. They'll be just fine! And just think how excited they'll be in the morning when you tell them the news. Children need a father.'

Marina nodded. 'I know.' She'd been the best kind of mother she could be, but already she was seeing Chakir blossom into boyhood under his father's guiding hand. Bahir would be a good father, she knew.

'Does he know about Hana yet?'

She shook her head, setting the large golden hoops in her ear dancing. It was her one last concern—that a man who did not really want a child he had not fathered would turn away that child when he discovered the girl was not even hers. 'Not yet. I didn't want to betray Sarah's confidence until I was sure. But I'll tell him first, so there can be no misunderstanding. Sarah would want me to.'

Catriona smiled and wished her luck, hugging her younger friend again. 'I'm so happy for you, Marina. If anyone deserves happiness, it's you.'

Tonight he was certain she would say yes. Tonight he was taking no chances. The luxurious tent complete with plunge pool he had ordered had been delivered and set up on a ridge overlooking a palm-filled valley, an unexpected treasure in the desert, a relic from dinosaur times and one he'd been saving for a special moment to share. That moment was now.

Bahir took in the scene as he waited for her, smiling at his cleverness, confident that after tonight it would be impossible to say no to him. Inside that plushly decorated and furnished tent, atop the cushioned bed and in the cooling waters of the crystal-clear plunge pool, he would set about making his final assault on her senses, his final step in persuading her to marry him.

Why she was holding out was a mystery when it was so clear that getting married was the right thing to do. The only thing to do.

Yes, he had treated her badly in the past—horrendously, he knew—but she understood the reasons why now. If she hadn't forgiven him, why was she so eager to share her body with him?

Because she wanted to be wooed?

He smiled as he surveyed the desert love-nest he had created, and waited for the car to bring her to him. So he would woo her tonight. Nothing would be left to chance. He had created the perfect place for them to escape to whenever they wanted. He had found a ring, set with an emerald the size of a bird's egg and surrounded by sparkling diamonds. He had found them the perfect house, in the same region of Italy, because she seemed to love it so much, but closer to Pisa to make travelling time between their two homes in Italy and Jaqbar easier. Idly he flicked through the property portfolio, passing time until he heard the sound of an engine in the distance and saw the headlights, and he shoved the brochure under a pile of towels and looked around one more time.

It was perfect.

He had left nothing to chance.

Together with the best sex in the universe, she would not be able to resist.

Tonight he could not fail.

Tonight she would be his.

She was sure it must be a mirage. They had travelled miles from the camp through nothingness, the moon obscured by a lonely cloud, when up ahead there appeared a strange red glow. A tent, she made out as they drew closer, a tent strung with colourful lanterns all around and a tall figure dressed all in white standing waiting outside.

Bahir.

Her pulse quickened. The sight of him in traditional robes, standing so straight and tall like one of the desert sheikhs of old, captured her imagination and stirred her senses. He looked so good in European clothes, in fine fabrics and designer-cut menswear, but in traditional robes he looked magnificent—a true Bedouin leader, standing there like a beacon in the dark.

She swallowed back on a delicious bubble of anticipation, glad she'd taken extra care with her own appearance tonight, her gold silk robe lavishly embroidered with intricate needlework and tiny precious stones that twinkled whenever she moved. She had known tonight would be special on so many levels. The effort Bahir had gone to to make it so proved it was for him too.

She smoothed her hands down the fabric, suddenly nervous. Tonight she would accept his proposal. Tonight she would agree to marry this man.

The car pulled up alongside the tent and Bahir stepped forward to open her door, his dark eyes glinting in the colours of the lanterns' warm glow. She accepted his hand and stepped from the car, and his eyes turned molten, warming her from the inside out. 'Welcome to my tent,' he said, and in the next breath, 'You look exquisite,' before nodding to the driver to leave them.

It was only then, when he had taken his eyes from her, that she noticed the pool behind him. The coloured light from the lamps played on the water and then beyond that the deep valley cut between the cliffs where palm trees sway grew thick and dense down the sides of the valley.

'What is this place?' she asked, taking a step towards the cliff.

'Palm Valley,' he said, wrapping his arms around her from behind, nuzzling at her neck. 'They say it has been here since the days of the dinosaurs. I think it was left here by the universe as a gift to you.'

She sighed as he warmed her skin with his mouth, setting it to tingling, already feeling the drugging effects of his caresses.

'And the tent and the pool?'

'Ah. That, now, is a gift to you from me.'

His hands flattened over her belly, one heading north to her breasts, cupping one in his fingers, his palm exquisite torture against one straining nipple, while the other headed south to cup the feminine mound at the apex of her thighs. She moaned softly as he pressed closer behind her, a reluctant protest, but knowing that there were things that must be said.

'I have refreshments,' he said. 'Sweetmeats with champagne, or sweet, spiced tea if you prefer.'

'No, nothing,' she said, knowing she must tell him about Hana, even as his hands stirred her desires until she felt herself grow slick with need. 'There's something I must do first…'

'I was hoping you'd feel that way,' he growled as he swung her into his arms. 'I can't wait either.'

She meant to stop him and make him put her down, but his mouth was already on hers and she was already too far gone, her senses buzzing, her body happily anticipating the pleasures to come. Besides, would it hurt to wait until after they'd made love to explain? He'd be more patient then, for a start, and most likely more receptive.

And afterwards she would tell him what she had decided—that she would marry him.

Maybe it was better to wait, she thought a few minutes later as his hot mouth blazed a trail up her inner thigh and his tongue flicked her *there*. Why spoil his fun when he was doing his best to persuade her?

Bahir was a master of persuasion, she reflected some indeterminable time later as she lay panting in the pool waiting for him to return with the promised tea. Even if she had come here tonight determined to say no to his proposal, by now she would be utterly convinced of the merits of marriage.

The bed he had laid her upon had just been the *entrée*. What he had dished up then had been a feast of sensual pleasure, a banquet designed to leave her giddy, knowing that it just didn't get any better. She smiled to herself. She would be marrying a man who made making love an art form. How lucky could one woman get?

And to make love to her like that—to worship her body so thoroughly—surely meant he must love her, she reasoned, even just a little. Otherwise she would make him love her. Once they were married.

Marina sighed, lingering in the star-kissed water one blissful moment longer, knowing it was late and that she should move.

Making love in a pool under the desert sky had been heaven but there was no putting off telling him about Hana any more. She would get dressed and tell him over tea and then, when he knew everything, if he still wanted to marry her, she would tell him yes. She groaned, feeling bone-weary after their night of sex, every muscle in her body protesting as she forced herself out of the pool and reached for one of the plush towels piled high on a side table.

The pile slid from the table to the ground, knocking something else off the table too, a mat of some kind. Not a mat, she realised, but a brochure, a real estate brochure. Curious, she wrapped the towel around herself, reached for it and started to read.

'You're out of the pool?'

She turned to see him bearing a tray with an ornate teapot, two tiny cups and a suspicious-looking box.

She looked up at him. 'I was in serious danger of falling asleep. Plus I needed to talk to you. I find I do that better when I'm not naked.' Though the way he looked right now, with a fluffy white towel slung low around his hips accentuating his dark-golden skin and making the most of the taper from his shoulders to his hips...

Maybe him looking naked would be less distracting. At least then she wouldn't have to use her imagination or resort to memories to peel it off…

She shook her head and held up the brochure, wondering if there would ever come a time when the mere sight of him didn't distract her. 'What's this?' she asked, holding it up so he could see. 'It was near the towels.'

'Ah,' he said, looking disappointed, pouring two cups of the sweetly scented brew, 'I was saving that for the finale, after you had agreed to marry me.'

A sizzle zipped down her spine.

So that explained the box on the tray…

Even though she had come here tonight knowing she would say yes to him, something about this latest surprise bothered her. Why was he thinking of buying such a place close to where she already lived in Tuscany, unless he wasn't planning on living with her once they were married? What kind of marriage was he contemplating? 'You are so sure that I would say yes?'

He smiled, looking almost boyish, and she couldn't help but see her son in his face. 'Of course you would say yes.'

She looked back at the brochure so she didn't have to answer beyond the rising tide of colour in her cheeks. Why did nothing suddenly making any sense? 'But I don't understand. What do you want with a house near Pisa?'

He moved to her shoulder and pointed to the pictures of the villa, the sprawling villa spread over several levels on fertile acreage, complete with infinity pool, tennis court and stables, all within fifteen minutes drive of Pisa. 'It's perfect, isn't it?'

Something about the way he said those words alerted her. 'It's lovely,' she said cautiously. Non-committally.

'And it's all down to you.' He put his arm around her shoulders, giving them a squeeze when she frowned up at him, not understanding. 'You were the one who pointed out I didn't even have a home to my name. Do you remember? And, given I have a son who needs a roof over his head, you were absolutely right.'

He pointed to something in the small print, something she could barely make out in the low lighting, not sure she would make sense of it even if the lights were brighter. 'Look where it is. I know you like the area, so I looked for something in the region, only closer to Pisa airport so that the commute between here and there doesn't take so long. I figured we would be spending some time here in Jaqbar as well.'

She held up one hand and shifted away. 'Hang on. What do you mean about Chakir needing a roof over his head? He has a perfectly good roof over his head where he is now.'

He shook his head dismissively. 'No. That is out of the question. I will not have my son living in a house that belongs to that man.'

'What man? Who do you mean?'

'Hana's father. I won't have my son living there.'

Something in her brain fused. She could not believe she had heard what she had just heard. 'What did you just say?'

'I said that my son will not live in a house owned by Hana's father. I am his father. From now on I will put a roof over my son's head. From now on, I will provide for him.'

'Who told you we lived in Hana's father's house?'

'Did you think I wouldn't work it out? A "good friend", you said. Who else could it be but a man only too happy to bury his mistake somewhere deep in the country where no one would ever find her?'

She reeled at his words as if he'd struck her a physical blow. She had suspected he would think the worst when she had told him the house belonged to a friend, but never had she imagined that he might concoct an entire fantasy around a throwaway line and assume it to be true. And she had thought she would never again hear him utter a certain word in the context of her children. 'I thought you knew better than to call either of my children a mistake.'

'I note you don't deny it is his house.'

'Only because it is too ridiculous to be true! Maybe this might convince you.' She slowed her delivery to one deliberate word at a time, hoping it might actually sink in. 'It—is—not—Hana's—father's—house. Satisfied?'

He blinked, then gave a toss of his head as if it didn't matter. 'It is of no consequence, you won't be needing it any more anyway.' He waved the brochure in the air. 'I will arrange to have everything packed and shipped before you leave the desert.'

She put a hand to her forehead, wondering when she had slipped into some parallel universe where Bahir had assumed ownership of her life. Maybe when she had cried out his name in pleasure or when she had dozed in the pool. And, while it would be so easy to set him straight and tell him the truth, this was not the way she had planned to tell him about Hana.

Besides, why should she have to explain at all? His

attitude alone was enough to make her dig her heels in. 'No, you will not do anything of the sort. Chakir has a home already. He is happy there. We all are. I'm sorry you went to all the trouble of buying a house when there is no need, but we have no intention of moving.'

He snorted his disgust and strode, hands on hips, beyond the pool to where the cliff edge fell away into the deep palm-filled valley. 'Why are you being so difficult about this?'

That was rich, coming from him. She was tired, even disappointed, that much was true. 'You think I'm the one being difficult?'

'If the house is so special, there must be a reason. And, if it is not Hana's father's, then whose house is it?' He looked over his shoulder at her, damnation in his eyes. 'Yet another of your lovers?'

Shock punched the air from her lungs. She, who'd been going to tell him tonight about Sarah and the arrangements she had put in place for her daughter, decided that she was glad she had said nothing before now. Because maybe she was getting a glimpse of the real Bahir, the man beneath the persuasive mask he'd been wearing all this week. 'What lovers? What are you talking about?'

'Come on, don't play the innocent. There must have been lovers after me. A woman with your appetites.'

'So what if there were? What about you? Have you had other lovers in the, oh, four years since we parted? Or have you nobly chosen to remain celibate in my honour? How touching! Then again, a man *with your appetites*?' she said, throwing his words right back at him and shaking her head knowingly. 'Somehow I very much doubt it.'

'There have been lovers,' he said, grinding the words out between his teeth. Of course there had been. Or, at least there had been sex. Nowhere near as much as she might think, and nowhere near as satisfying as it should have been, not that she needed to know either of those facts. 'At least I am willing to admit it.'

'What do you want, Bahir? A blow-by-blow description of my life after you threw me out? No! You abrogated all rights to the intimate details of my life when you told me to get out of your life and that you never wanted to see me again.'

Then she seemed to wilt before him, the fire in her eyes extinguished. She put her hands to her face on a sigh. 'And we know why you said that now, don't we? We know why you banished me from your life that day.'

She shook her head, looking up at him plaintively, her dark eyes almost too big for her face. 'Oh God, what's happening here, Bahir? Why are you doing this? Why are we arguing?'

For a moment he didn't know why and he knew even less how to answer. How had they got to this place? And what did he really want? A guarantee that if he gambled on this marriage, that he wouldn't end up the loser? How could anyone give such a guarantee? When had he ever expected one of those?

But he needed to know the odds.

'I just want you to tell me the truth.'

She gave a weak laugh. 'The truth.' She held out her arms by her side and dropped them again. 'Now, there's a concept. Okay, so maybe it's time you heard the truth. Maybe this time you'll be ready to believe it. I love you, Bahir, with all my heart and all my soul. There was never anyone else. There never has been.'

The gears in his brain crunched to a standstill with all he knew and with all he had seen. 'Is that what you told Hana's father?'

She didn't answer. She just looked up at him with those damned eyes that made him almost hurt to look at them, as though she was the one who was wronged. And then she simply said, 'I want to go home.'

She wasn't getting out of it that easily. 'I saw you,' he said. 'A month after we split up I saw you in Monte Carlo. You were wearing that red dress that I'd bought you, the one I loved peeling off. And you were with a man...'

She just closed her eyes and shook her head. 'I want to go home.'

He sighed wearily and looked upwards, seeing the sky and the stars sliding lower on the horizon, recognising that in a few short hours it would be dawn. Recognising that there was no time to fix this now. 'Get dressed,' he said gruffly, looking at the tray with the ring box still sitting there untouched, angry that the night that had started out with such promise had ended so badly. And all because he'd stupidly put the brochure somewhere she could find it. But why did she take offence every time he mentioned Hana's father? Why did she try to pretend the affair had never happened?

'I'll take you back to the camp. We can talk about this later.'

'No,' she said, turning her body away from him, dragging on her clothes as quickly as she could. 'I want to go home. I want to go anywhere that's as far from you as I can possibly get.'

He reached out and touched a hand to her shoulder to turn her. 'Marina, don't do this—'

'Don't touch me!' She shrugged out of his grasp. 'Don't you ever lay a finger on me again.'

'Marina!'

She pulled her robe over her head, lifting out the curtain of her long black hair as she swung around. 'And you know the funny thing in all this? The thing that really cracks me up?'

When it came, his voice was as dry as the desert sands. 'Tell me, if you must.'

She swiped up one sandal from the floor and shoved it on her foot. 'I never even met Hana's father. How's that for a laugh?'

'What are you saying?'

'You work it out, Bahir,' she said, searching for her other sandal. 'You, who thinks he knows so much about who I sleep with and how often.'

'Marina—'

'Oh, and the really funny one? You'll get a good belly laugh out of this one, I promise you: Hana owns the house. Not her father or some other mythical lover from that long list you seem to want to attribute to me, but Hana.' She gave a mock frown. 'But you're not laughing, Bahir. Don't you think it's funny?'

She wasn't making any sense. 'How can Hana own a house?'

'Simple. Her mother left it to her. Now, get me out of this hellhole desert fantasy of yours and then get us to Souza. I'm taking my children home.'

He wasn't laughing. Instead, as he drove back to camp with Marina staring blankly out of the passenger window feigning interest in the inky darkness, he felt like the world as he knew it was coming apart at the seams.

And, battle as he might, he could not get the pieces to fit back together again. Not in any way that fitted with what he knew.

Because she had professed her love to him in one breath and fallen into someone else's arms the next.

Hadn't she?

She had borne his child and gone on to have another's in the blink of an eye.

Hadn't she?

She had been living all this time in the house of her sometime lover.

But then she had said it was Hana's house.

Oh God. These assumptions were the very foundation of his treatment of her all along. These formed the cornerstones of his resentment. How he had resented the way she had moved on so quickly—how that belief had poisoned his mind and turned this night toxic.

And if those assumptions were wrong…

Her words jumbled in his head. *Hana's house. Her mother.* A father Marina had never met. How could any of it make sense? The four-wheel drive tore over the rocky desert track just as realisation sliced through his senses like a scythe.

Unless Hana was someone else's child.

There was no other explanation. Why had he been so blind all this time? Because, apart from her dark hair, she didn't even look like Marina.

Except he knew why he had been blind all this time—because it had been what he had wanted to believe. To prove he hadn't made a mistake all those years ago. To put a lid on his feelings for her and label them with a very different emotion. To protect himself from life's greatest gamble.

Except now he had lost everything.

He had lost her.

There was nothing to see in the inky darkness on the way back to the camp except for the eerie glow from the eyes of a night creature caught in the spotlights before slinking away. There was nothing to say, and if Bahir was curious he didn't let on—which was good, because Marina wasn't inclined to fill him in on the details of how Hana had come to own their villa in Tuscany. He could construct his own explanation. He was a master at that.

Besides, she felt too gutted to speak. There was nothing inside her but a yawning pit into which all her stupid, pointless hopes and dreams had fallen, smashing to dust when they hit rock bottom. Instead she fixed her gaze out of the passenger window and watched the night sky peel away, layer by layer, preparing for the coming dawn, and felt the first stirrings of maternal unease.

What had she been thinking? All those pointless, fruitless hours she had spent with him, thinking this was *the* night, allowing herself to be seduced, imagining it could possibly end in happiness.

What a fool she'd been.

What a damned, stupid fool.

They topped the last rise and a blaze of lights shone

in the distance, bright where surely there should be no more than a lamp or two.

'What's that?' she asked, that curling ribbon of unease snaking and twisting inside her.

'The camp,' he said, putting his foot down on the accelerator, and the feeling of unease in her stomach became a full-blown fear.

She should never have left.

They pulled up in a flurry of dust and stones only to be greeted by the tear-streaked face of Catriona, Chakir clutched tightly in her arms, his dark eyes looking bewildered at the fuss.

'It's Hana,' she said. 'We can't find her.'

CHAPTER ELEVEN

'No!' Ice ran through Marina's veins as she bolted from the car and raced into their tent, needing to see for herself Hana's empty bed. The sheets were cold to the touch when she rested the palm of her hand down on them.

Oh God, she thought, feeling sick. She should never have gone. Why had she gone? Why had she stayed away so long? 'How long has she been missing?' she asked, taking Chakir from the distressed Catriona, needing to hug him, to prove one of her children was still there. 'Where have they looked?'

'I'm so sorry,' Catriona said, distraught. 'She must have slipped out while I was asleep. I don't know how long she's been gone.'

'She can't have gone far,' Marina said, wishing for it to be so.

'They're looking through every tent again. Searchers have started fanning out into the desert in case she wandered off.'

'No!' She collapsed into a chair, clutching Chakir tightly to her chest, her hand cradling his head. He was too big now to be held that way and he squirmed under her hands, but she would not let him go. The thought of Hana wandering off into the dark desert night over shifting desert sands was too dreadful to contemplate.

'I'll find her,' she heard Bahir say, but his voice sounded a long way away.

'I wish I hadn't gone,' she said, rocking her son. 'I should never have gone. I should never have left them.'

He watched her while she rocked, her face bleached white with shock, her arms wound so tightly around their son that he could feel her pain. 'I'll find her,' he repeated as much for his own benefit as for hers.

After the mess he had made of tonight, he had to.

The camp was alive with activity when he emerged from the tent, everyone aware of the seriousness of the situation; of a tiny child, wandering lost and alone in the desert. She couldn't have gone far, he rationalised as he threw the brightly coloured Arabian saddle over his horse, not on her short legs. But, still, which way had she gone? If anything happened to her, she would never forgive herself for leaving the children and he would never forgive himself for taking her away from them.

The sky was lightening now, the promise of a new day also a threat, bringing a scorching sun to the hunt, both a blessing and a curse.

His mount snorted and hoofed the earth, as if sensing the urgency as he leapt onto its back and wheeled it around, preparing to set off. Where would a child go? he wondered, scanning the surrounding dunes now lit with half-light. Where would Hana go?

He had already headed to the top of the nearest dune when he heard the goat bleating, an oddly discordant note to its sound. He turned his mount around and looked more closely at the flock of animals contained in a loose corral. It sounded almost as if something was wrong.

And he wondered.

Animals scattered as he came close, the black Bedouin goats and desert sheep waking in alarm, bleating protests at the stranger in their midst as they skittered out of his way. Then he saw the old mother goat lying at the back, blinking up at him with her sideways eyes, her twin kids nestled together on the ground, a tiny child curled in their midst.

A motionless child.

Hana!

He must have said her name out loud because she woke with a start and burst into tears, confused and disoriented as he lifted her to his chest. And he was so relieved that she was all right, that she had only been asleep, that he just held her and cuddled her close and told her it was all right, even as she wailed against his chest and cried for her mother.

'It's okay, Hana. I'll take you to your mother,' he said, rubbing her back the way he'd seen Marina do, talking to the child in a low voice, hoping to calm her down. 'She was worried about you, and so sorry she wasn't there. That was my fault. I took her away. I should never have done that.'

The child's sobs slowed. She curled closer to him, recognising him, feeling safer. 'And if anything had happened to you,' he said, stroking her hair as her head rested on his shoulder, 'I would never have forgiven myself. You have a special mother, you know, and she deserves better than anything I can give her. Much better. Just as you deserve a father who can keep you safe.'

Hana sniffed against his shoulder and rubbed her eyes and he leaned his head down and kissed her black curls. 'But I will miss you, Hana Banana, when you are gone. And it will be my own stupid fault, for not realising how precious your mother was from the very beginning. For never being able to tell her what I felt because I didn't understand what I felt. For being jealous of shadows. For never realising all this time that I loved her. Only now it's too late.'

'Hana,' she said, looking up at him solemnly as she focused on the important part of his conversation. 'Hana 'nana.'

He smiled in spite of the dampness he felt rising in his eyes, knowing he had missed a chance at life and love. Knowing he was returning to a bleak and pointless future—the future of his own making, the future he *deserved*—and now all the more bleak for knowing what he would be missing. 'You are,' he said, touching a fingertip to the tip of her cute nose, 'the best Hana 'nana ever.'

She giggled and he smiled with her, even as he felt his own world crumbling apart.

The goats! Marina was sitting with Chakir on her lap when she wondered—had anyone checked the goats? She kissed her son and left him with Catriona, who promised a hundred times that she would not take her eyes from him. Marina hugged her and told her to stop blaming herself and ran from the tent.

Hana was in love with those baby goats. Had anyone looked? Was there a chance?

She heard her daughter's screams before she got

there and she almost bolted across the sands towards the sound in relief, until she saw Bahir with his back to her, cradling Hana against his shoulder, his soothing hand at her back; until she heard the words he uttered to her and she paused silent in the cool light of dawn to listen.

'My fault,' she heard him say amongst the snippets of his words she could catch. 'She deserves better.' So true, she thought, knowing she must remain resolute and equally determined not to have her intentions to return home watered down by the picture of him cradling Hana on his shoulder, a picture she had dreamed of happening one day—lots of one days. But why did it have to happen now?

Why now, when everything was lost?

She would have stepped from the shadows then— she almost did—except she heard him say, 'And it will be my own stupid fault, for not realising how precious your mother was from the very beginning.' She paused, and heard him go on to talk of jealousy and shadows, then of love—she held her breath—and of how it was now too late.

Her lungs sucked in air. She must have made a sound, because Hana lifted her head from his shoulder and saw her. 'Mama!' she cried, holding out her arms.

She ran to her child then, scooping her from his arms and hugged her close. 'Oh, Hana, you gave me such a scare. What were you doing here with your goats?'

'Goat,' Hana said, pointing to the babies now drinking at their mother's teats, and she looked up, saw Bahir standing there and smiled. 'Thank you,' she said.

He gave a slight bow of his head. Formally. Distantly.

As if he had already withdrawn from her, knowing she was leaving. 'I will make arrangements for your departure to Souza.'

She knew she should still go home. She had made up her mind to go. But something about his softly spoken words made her hesitate. No, not something—his talk of love made her hesitate. Made her wonder...

'There's no rush,' she said, and he looked back at her, confusion skating across the surface of his dark eyes. 'Hana will need to rest. We all will.'

As if on cue, Hana yawned and dropped her head onto her mother's shoulder. He nodded and turned to go. 'Of course. Whenever you are ready. I will go and call off the search.'

'And Bahir?'

He stopped but this time he didn't turn around. 'Can we talk?' she said. 'Once Hana is asleep? I was going to tell you last night before... Well, I didn't tell you, and I owe you an explanation at least.'

He shook his head, looking down at his feet. 'You owe me nothing. Not after what I have done to you. The things I have said...'

The note of despair in his flat lifeless voice squeezed her heart. 'Come to my tent once you have called off the search and I will tell you about my friend Sarah.' She looked down at the drowsy child in her arms. 'Hana's birth mother.'

Hana was sleeping when he lifted the flap into the children's sleeping quarters a little while later, Marina sitting alongside and watching her as if she was afraid she might disappear again. Though she didn't turn, she must have sensed it was him, because without looking his way she gestured him to enter and sit down on the end of the bed.

'Sarah was a friend of mine,' she started as he sat down softly. 'I'd met her a few times at the casino and we'd say hello, but it was after our split that we grew closer.' She looked over at him then, a sad smile on her face. 'She helped me, you see, in the days and weeks following— Well, you know. She let me move in with her, and when she found out I was pregnant she mothered me a little. She had always wanted a baby, she said. She wanted nothing more in the world. But she had suffered from cancer as a teenager and wasn't sure she even could conceive a child.

'And then Chakir was born and she decided she wanted a baby more than ever, while there still might be a slim chance she might be a mother. She didn't have a partner and so she found a nameless man—I never found out who, I never knew the details—and became pregnant.'

She sniffed, and he could see the glow of moisture in her eyes. 'It was while they were doing the pregnancy tests that they found out the cancer was back, and this time more aggressive than ever. They told her she would have to have an abortion, because the treatment she needed to save her would kill her baby.'

She pressed her lips together. 'She refused treatment. She wanted this baby so much, even though she knew the risk to herself. Even though she knew it might well cost her own life, she knew she would never get another chance. And when Hana was born she said it was the happiest day of her life, even though her body was wasted and she was already dying and there was nothing the doctors could do…'

Her voice trailed away as the tears rolled down her cheeks and he ached to kiss them away, but he knew he had no right to touch her or to soothe her pain when he had caused so much of it himself, pain he now knew was so wrongfully inflicted. He had no right to comfort her.

'She loved Hana so much,' she continued, her hands clenched tightly in her lap. 'And she asked me if I would adopt her, because she wanted Hana and Chakir to grow up together.'

'She had no family of her own?'

'Sarah was estranged from her parents—they were very strict and they cut her off when they learned she was working in a casino. I don't know what they thought she did there, but they said they preferred to think that she'd died of her cancer rather than live with the eternal shame of knowing she worked in such a "den of iniquity". Only her grandmother kept in touch. It hurt Sarah terribly, but it made her stronger too, and more determined to experience everything that she could.

'And then her grandmother died and left her enough money to buy the house in Tuscany. A refuge, she called it, her sanctuary. And when her parents argued the money should be theirs, she told them it was already gone and they assumed she'd gambled it away.'

She sighed and looked down at the hands in her lap.

'She left it to Hana. She wanted her to always have a home, for us all to have a home. And nobody blinked when I emerged from the Tuscan mountainside with another baby to my name. Nobody questioned that the party-girl princess had been irresponsible again.'

Guilt consumed him. He hung his head in shame and horror at the assumptions he had made—at the sheer injustice of them.

'I promised Sarah I would tell nobody our secret. Only Catriona and the lawyers knew and that's how it would stay.' She shook her head. 'She never told me who Hana's father was and I never asked, but Sarah was more afraid of her parents and what they might do if they discovered the truth. So I promised Sarah I would look after Hana as my own. I promised I would keep her safe and never betray her trust.'

He should have seen it coming. He should have guessed. Because hadn't he noticed? Hadn't he remarked on it himself? Hadn't he infused her answer with yet more damnation? 'You have no idea if she looks like her father, do you?'

This time Marina smiled, her liquid eyes glowing with the memories of her friend. 'She's the image of Sarah. She's beautiful.'

'I was so wrong,' he said, knowing his words to be painfully inadequate. Knowing they were nowhere near enough. Knowing he could never make up for all the wrongs he'd committed against this warm, wonderful woman who had taken another woman's child and nurtured it as her own. 'I am so sorry, Marina.'

She shrugged and gave a wan smile. 'That day you saw me, in the casino, in your red dress—there were four of us that night. It was Sarah's birthday and she convinced me to go out and wear that dress while I still could, while it still fit.'

The lamp on the tent wall flickered as she sighed. 'I didn't want to go. I didn't want to party, I didn't want any chance of seeing you. But you'd said something about going to Macau, and besides, it was Sarah's birthday and I wanted to be happy for her. She deserved to be happy. But I don't even remember who that man was. I'd never met him before. I never met him again. I went home early that night...'

God. He dropped his head into his hands. 'You must hate me,' he said. 'I don't blame you for hating me. I hate myself for the things I have said to you. For my toxic thoughts and words.'

'I wanted to. I still want to.' She swung her head his way then, a tiny frown between her dark brows. 'Why were you there that night, when you had said you were leaving Europe? Why did you come back?'

He snorted out a laugh. 'I came looking for you. I wanted...' He thought back to that night, to the torture of a month of regret and self-damnation. 'I wanted to tell you I was sorry.' And this time he did manage to laugh, a derisive, self-deprecating laugh. 'The pattern of my life, it seems—apologising to you for treating you so appallingly.'

'You came back to find me?'

'I'd had a month to think about the things I'd said to you in anger. I'd tried to put it out of my mind, but I could not forgive myself. I thought, if I found you and explained, that you might understand and maybe even forgive me yourself.

'Except my anger rose anew when I saw you smiling and laughing, like I had never existed. I told myself I was a fool for thinking you would want me back. I told myself I was a fool for thinking that I wanted your love—that I loved you too.

'God, what a mess.' He rose, raking his fingers through his hair. 'I'm sorry, Marina. I know it's no consolation, but I will never stop being sorry for the way I have treated you.'

'You came back to find me? To tell me you were sorry?' She couldn't get her head around it. The fact he had come back. The fact he had wanted her back. And it was suddenly too much bear—the thought of all these wasted years, all the pointless grief. She dropped her head into her hands as fresh tears flooded her eyes. All that futile, pointless grief.

She felt his strong arms go around her, wrapping her into his embrace. 'I'm so sorry,' he whispered hoarsely, rocking her as she had seen him do with Hana such a short time ago.

'I want to hate you,' she said. 'Because I was prepared to walk away.' She sniffed, sobbing. 'And now you tell me you loved me. Now, when it's too late.'

He drew her to her feet, smoothing the tears from her cheeks with the pads of his thumbs. 'You are better off without me. You are better off going home and forgetting you ever met me. You are better off hating me.'

'But I can't.' She sniffed, grinding the words through her teeth, curling her hands into fists and jamming them in between them, pounding at the solid wall of his chest to stress her words. 'I tried and I tried. But, damn you, I can't!'

'Then try harder. Remember all the things I did and said. Because I am a bad bet, Marina. I will never be good enough for you. You deserve better.' He turned to go, was already out of Hana's room when she caught him, and clamped her hands around his before he could walk out of her life for the second time.

'I don't want better,' she protested. 'I want you, Bahir. I love you. I can't stop loving you. And you told Hana. I heard you. You told her that you loved me.'

He stilled. 'You heard me say that?'

'You told her, I heard you. And now I want you to tell me. Surely I deserve to hear it?'

He looked into her eyes, searching them, almost hopeful, until he blinked and the despair returned to colour their depths. 'What good can it possibly do? There is no point to this, Marina. I have done enough harm. I will not hurt you any more. I will not risk it.'

'I want to hear the words, Bahir. If you are truly sorry, then tell me what I have longed to hear for so long. You owe it to me.'

And this time he hesitated only a moment before he wrapped her in his arms and crushed her to his chest. 'Oh, my love, my sweet, sweet love. I do love you, Marina, and I hate myself for causing you so much pain. I will never forgive myself.'

She sagged against him, relief and hope washing through her. At last the words she'd longed to hear. 'I forgive you. If that helps.'

He took her face in his hands, his eyes looking down at her with a mix of helplessness and hope. 'How can you ever forgive me?'

'Because I love you, Bahir. I have always loved you. Don't you understand? There was never going to be anyone else. There couldn't be.'

'But you are too good for me. You deserve better.'

She pushed away from his chest to look up at him.

'No! Listen, Bahir, why do you think it suited me to take Hana? Do you think I did it purely out of the goodness of my heart? Of course, I would have done anything for Sarah, but it suited me too. For no man would be tempted to get involved with me, the mother of two illegitimate children, for fear that they might end up lumbered with us all. Don't you see? They protected me. I used them to hide behind, just as I used Sarah's house as my own sanctuary. It kept me safely tucked away, where nobody could find me. Where nobody could get close.

'The same with you,' she admitted. 'Because I let you think there was another man or other men. I let you believe what you wanted about who owned the house— out of spite at first, it's true, because you seemed too ready to believe the worst of me. And then it was easier to let you keep believing it. I'm so sorry. But I used Hana as a defence against you. I used her as a reason to hate you. I didn't tell you she wasn't mine only because I'd promised Sarah, but because it suited me to let you think I'd been with someone else, if only as some kind of defence against what I really felt for you. If only like some kind of protection.'

'You shouldn't need protection,' he said, pulling her close, stroking her hair. 'You should have someone to protect you. You should not be alone. You deserve to be loved.'

She breathed in, relishing his warm, masculine scent. 'You're so right, Bahir. I deserve to be loved. Which is why I have to ask you…'

His heart skipped a beat under her ear. 'Ask me what?'

She smiled up at him. 'I'm asking if you will do me the honour of becoming my husband?'

He pushed her away at arm's length. 'You would still marry me? After all that I have said and done?'

'Only if you really wanted to. Only if you would take us all—me, Chakir and Hana—and promise to love us for ever. Promise to make us one family.'

He breathed in, raising his face to the ceiling, before he looked back at her, incredulous. 'Whatever did I do in this world to deserve you? When did luck ever deal a better hand? Because yes, Marina, I will marry you. I will be your husband and I promise that you will never be sorry.'

'I know,' she said, a rush of happiness sweeping through her as she raised her lips for his kiss. 'I'm betting on it.'

EPILOGUE

THEY were married twice. Once in Jaqbar in the desert in the traditional way—a 'simple' three-day ceremony filled with much feasting, music and celebration—and once again in Jemeya, this time a fusion of East and West, and held in the palace of her father, the King, and her childhood home.

Chakir solemnly bore the rings on a golden cushion, his dark eyes concentrating on the pillow and so serious as he walked towards the altar that he looked like a mini-Bahir.

Hana followed, their tiny flower girl, looking beautiful in a frothy white dress with a circlet of flowers on her black hair, one gloved hand wrapped around her tiny posy, the other tucked into the hand of her beautiful aunt Aisha who whispered words of encouragement as the wide-eyed child took faltering steps down the aisle.

Marina watched her tiny toddler gait with a bittersweet smile on her face, wishing Sarah could be here to see how much she'd grown, and how beautiful she looked with her hair done up and with the coiled ringlets framing her face.

As her father told her it was time and they set off down the aisle behind them, and she looked beyond her sister and her daughter, she saw Bahir at the front along-side his three friends, Zoltan, Rashid and Kadar, his dark eyes on Hana, his eyes smiling as she approached. He looked up then, and across the distance their eyes snagged and held and she felt the familiar sizzle all the way down to her toes.

Her father patted her hand as he walked her down the aisle. 'He's a fine man you're marrying.'

She only half-turned towards him, nodding to the guests as they passed. 'I know, Papa.'

'And I just wanted to tell you,' he continued, his voice low and gruff, 'that I'm proud of you, Marina. I know we've had our differences in the past, but I just want you to know that.'

This time when she looked across at him she was surprised to see he had tears in his eyes. 'Oh, Papa!' Even as they continued up the aisle, she reached up and pressed her lips to his cheek. 'I love you too.'

Her father beamed with pride and squeezed her hand tighter. 'Two daughters married,' he said as he passed her hand to Bahir's. 'To two fine men. Can it get any better?'

Marina looked up at Bahir as her father passed her hand to his, saw the man she intended spending the rest of her life with form the word 'beautiful' with his lips, and thought with a secret smile, maybe it could, but that would wait just a little while longer.

First of all, she had a man to marry.

Her heart sang as they took their vows. Chakir proffered up the cushion bearing their rings and Bahir slipped the twisted band of tricolour gold onto her fin-ger—white-gold for the endless desert plains, yellow-gold for the sun and rose-gold for sunrise and the promise of a new day.

He slipped the ring onto her finger before lifting it to his mouth and kissing it. 'I love you,' he whispered, a totally unexpected gesture that made her wish they were a million miles away and somewhere private instead of standing in front of a crowded room where every eye was upon them.

Then the ceremony was over and he surprised her again, scooping Hana into his arms before he slipped his arm through hers to walk down the aisle behind Chakir as the guests broke into spontaneous applause. Aboard Bahir's shoulder, Hana clapped her hands and giggled, delighted. She looked up at him, wondering. 'But what…?'

'Chakir and I had it all organised, didn't we, Chakir?' And their son looked over his shoulder and grinned up at her, nodding. 'We're a fambily now.'

'That's right,' said Bahir with a smile at Chakir's mispronuncination. 'We're a family. We should do this together.'

Their formal reception soon became a celebration, and at one stage it seemed everyone was on the dance floor, Bahir with Marina, Zoltan with Aisha and even Chakir dancing with Hana, the two of them spinning until they collapsed in fits of giggles on the dance floor.

Rashid and Kadar watched on from the side, Zoltan and Bahir joining them during a break.

'It looks like Zoltan's set a trend,' Bahir said, sporting the gold band on his finger. 'That's two out of four of us married so far. Who's next?'

Kadar and Rashid took a long look at each other.

'Don't look at me,' they both said together, and Bahir and Zoltan both laughed.

'Don't be so sure of that. You just never know.'

'What's the big joke?' asked Marina as the two women joined the men. Bahir moved to her side, unable to resist slipping his arm proprietorially around his new wife's slender waist in case anyone else thought of asking for the next dance before he could.

'Zoltan and I are laying odds on which one of these two jokers is next for the marriage stakes.'

'Not a chance,' said Rashid, holding up his hands. 'Once a playboy, always a playboy.'

'Besides,' Kadar joined in. 'All the good women are taken.'

'You better believe it,' Bahir said, whisking his bride off for another spin around the dance floor, closely followed by Aisha and Zoltan.

'Did I tell you,' Bahir started as he pulled her close in his embrace, 'just how beautiful you look today?'

Marina smiled. 'Oh, maybe a dozen times, no more than that.'

'I knew I hadn't said it anywhere near enough. You are the most beautiful woman I've ever seen, today more than ever.'

'Because you make me the happiest woman alive, Bahir.'

They kissed in the midst of the dance floor while Zoltan and Aisha spun by with eyes only for each other, the love they felt for each other clearly on display. Bahir smiled when he looked at them. 'To think Chakir and Hana will soon have a new playmate when Zoltan and Aisha's baby arrives. They will like that.'

She smiled up at him. 'Maybe two.'

'They're having twins? Zoltan didn't say.'

'No. Not twins. But there's another baby coming. Another playmate for Chakir and Hana.'

He stopped dancing, his heart skipping a beat, holding her at arm's length to look at her. 'You mean you…? We…? You mean…?'

She laughed. 'I mean we are having a baby, Bahir.'

'But when? How?'

Her smile was softer this time as she stepped back into his warm embrace. 'In the desert where we lay together that day. We have been sent a blessing from your family and from your tribe. We have been sent a blessing in the form of a child.'

He pulled her to him then, wrapping her in his arms, pressing his lips to her head as a joy so profound filled him until it spilled over and coloured the world in rich harmonious light. And when he could breathe again, when he could think, he lifted her chin with his hand and saw the moisture in her eyes, moisture that mirrored his own.

'You have made me the happiest man alive, Marina. You have given back something to me I thought was lost for ever. You have given me back my family. I love you so much.'

'As I love you, Bahir. As I will always love you.'

There were no words he could find to answer her, there were no words that could prove what he said to be true. So he told her with his kiss as they spun together on the dance floor, just as he would prove it every day of their life together.

* * * * *

So you think you can write?

**Mills & Boon® and Harlequin®
have joined forces in a
global search for new authors.**

It's our biggest contest yet—with the prize
of being published by the world's
leader in romance fiction.

Look for more information on our website:
www.soyouthinkyoucanwrite.com

So you think you can write?
Show us!

A sneaky peek at next month...

MODERN™

INTERNATIONAL AFFAIRS, SEDUCTION & PASSION GUARANTEED

My wish list for next month's titles...

In stores from 17th August 2012:

❏ Unlocking her Innocence − Lynne Graham

❏ His Reputation Precedes Him − Carole Mortimer

❏ Just One Last Night − Helen Brooks

❏ The Husband She Never Knew − Kate Hewitt

In stores from 7th September 2012:

❏ Santiago's Command − Kim Lawrence

❏ The Price of Retribution − Sara Craven

❏ The Greek's Acquisition − Chantelle Shaw

❏ When Only Diamonds Will Do − Lindsay Armstrong

❏ The Couple Behind the Headlines − Lucy King

Available at WHSmith, Tesco, Asda, Eason, Amazon and Apple

Just can't wait?

MILLS & BOON® Book Club

2 Free Books!

Get your free books now at
www.millsandboon.co.uk/freebookoffer

Or fill in the form below and post it back to us

THE MILLS & BOON® BOOK CLUB™—HERE'S HOW IT WORKS: Accepting your free books places you under no obligation to buy anything. You may keep the books and return the despatch note marked 'Cancel'. If we do not hear from you, about a month later we'll send you 4 brand-new stories from the Modern™ series priced at £3.49* each. There is no extra charge for post and packaging. You may cancel at any time, otherwise we will send you 4 stories a month which you may purchase or return to us—the choice is yours. *Terms and prices subject to change without notice. Offer valid in UK only. Applicants must be 18 or over. Offer expires 31st January 2013. **For full terms and conditions, please go to www.millsandboon.co.uk/freebookoffer**

Mrs/Miss/Ms/Mr (please circle)
_____

First Name
_____

Surname
_____

Address
_____

_____

                                            Postcode
_____

E-mail
_____

Send this completed page to: Mills & Boon Book Club, Free Book Offer, FREEPOST NAT 10298, Richmond, Surrey, TW9 1BR

Find out more at
www.millsandboon.co.uk/freebookoffer

Visit us Online

0712/P2YEA

A